ONE DAY AT A TIME

ONE DAY
AT A TIME

Julie Ellis

This first world edition published in Great Britain 2005 by
SEVERN HOUSE PUBLISHERS LTD of
9–15 High Street, Sutton, Surrey SM1 1DF.
This first world edition published in the USA 2005 by
SEVERN HOUSE PUBLISHERS INC of
595 Madison Avenue, New York, N.Y. 10022.

British Library Cataloguing in Publication Data

Ellis, Julie, 1933-
    One day at a time
    1.   Middle aged women - Fiction
    2.   Married people - Psychology - Fiction
    I.   Title
    813.5'4 [F]

    ISBN 0-7278-6194-8

Typeset by Palimpsest Book Production Ltd.,
Polmont, Stirlingshire, Scotland.
Printed and bound in Great Britain by
MPG Books Ltd., Bodmin, Cornwall.

For Susie and Richie, my treasures

One

Claudia Adams – short dark hair becomingly styled, the dramatic blue of her eyes accentuated by her turquoise designer pantsuit – glanced about the restaurant. Not an empty table in Michael's at the height of the lunch hour. For years the New York publishing world had anointed Michael's as one of its 'in' restaurants. Their table – in an obscure corner of the room – indicated their lack of stature in the world of New York publishing. This was of no concern to Claudia. She'd chosen Michael's because she knew this would please Daisy – for fourteen years an editor and now a literary agent. Daisy had flown from San Francisco for this occasion – using the trip as a business venture as well. *'Tax-deductible, you know.'*

Claudia viewed the other four women who comprised the self-styled 'Fantastic Five' with a sense of nostalgia for the college years that gave birth to their title. It seemed incredible that they'd graduated college twenty-two years ago this past May. Each with grandiose visions of the future that lay ahead for her.

Once a year they met for a reunion in the host-of-the-year's home town. Always on the third Friday of October. This was her year to host. She knew the tab for today's luncheon would be high, but then the others expected to dine well. They were all aware of Todd's soaring success in investment banking. Last year – Shirley's host year – they'd driven all the way from her Long Island community up to Gurney's Inn in Montauk for lunch, afterwards walked on the beach with a

1

sense of regained youth. She'd reimbursed Shirley for the Gurney's tab.

Shirley and she had been roommates all through college, had seen each other regularly through the years. Shirley was godmother to Jill and Larry, as she was to Shirley's Scott and Annie. She'd married right out of college. Shirley waited until she was thirty and sharply aware that her biological clock was ticking away. Scott was eleven, Annie nine.

'I tell you, divorcing my rat of a husband was the best thing I ever did.' Daisy's voice brought Claudia back to the moment. 'My mother expected me to go into a decline,' she drawled. 'The last five years have been the best. I loved editing – and now I love being a literary agent. I work my butt off,' she conceded, 'and I have some real cliffhangers. But I wouldn't do anything else.'

'Bob and I have had some bad moments—' Beth was momentarily somber. 'But we both worked our way through law school and into a profession that's been fairly good financially. We would have liked to have had kids,' she said with candor. 'But it didn't happen. We're still building career-wise – and who knows? One day we may hit the jackpot.' She turned to Claudia. 'Like you and Todd,' she joshed, and Claudia sensed an undertone of envy. Beth and her husband lived and practiced corporate law in a medium-sized town in Pennsylvania. In those early years – before she married – Beth had talked about a partnership in a major New York firm, exciting criminal cases. She'd been shocked and furious to discover that men in her firm – doing the same work as she – earned far more. *'And no way can I break through that glass ceiling.'*

'Todd works like a demon.' *Why do I feel self-conscious about his success?* 'We've lived in six states in the twenty-two years we've been married.' *But they know this.* 'I see so little of him – the kids saw so little of him during their growing-up years. That bothered me.' *But I was a 'stay-at-home mom'. I was always there for them.*

Jill was twenty-one and fresh out of college – sharing an

apartment with a college friend. Larry a sophomore in an Ivy League college. Claudia forced a smile. To the others Todd and she were the Successful Couple. Long weekends in the Caribbean in the winter, a rented house in the Hamptons in the summer. They hadn't bought. Todd had dismissed this right away. *'Who needs the responsibilities of taking care of a house? It's easier to rent.'*

'But now you're settled in Manhattan.' Lois – the only other one of their tightly knit group who'd married early, and was the mother of four – noted wistfully. 'And you have that gorgeous condo in the West Village. I'd love to live in the heart of Boston, but with the rents – and condo prices – fierce, we know we have to stay in suburbia. Thank God, we bought a house before the prices went berserk – but I dread to think of college costs for four. It's rough with one just starting.'

'College is far off for Scott and Annie. I don't want to think what it'll cost when they're ready.' Shirley shuddered. 'Though my going back to work part-time once both were in school helped,' she conceded. They all knew that Bill's guidance counselor salary provided security but no luxuries. Shirley was somber for a moment. 'I'm not sure I should have waited so long to get back in the job market. Twelve bucks an hour doesn't thrill me.'

It was absurd for her to feel guilty that Todd did so well financially, Claudia told herself. None of them could be listed as one of the *New York Times'* '100 Neediest.' Out of college she and Todd had both been filled with a need to go out into the world and 'make a difference.'

For a wistful moment she remembered their determination to join the Peace Corps. All the research they did! Both pairs of parents had been fearful of this – and then she got pregnant.

Somewhere along the way they got lost, she thought with rare candor. She ought to be thrilled with their lifestyle. But she was forever conscious of something lacking. For a long time. Todd had changed in so many ways. Sometimes she felt as though she was living with a stranger.

3

After consuming a fabulous dessert and lingering over coffee, they said their good-byes and traveled off in different directions. Daisy to her hotel to meet with a prospective client. Beth to catch a train back home. Lois was meeting a cousin who lived in Queens and would spend the night with her before heading back for Boston. Claudia and Shirley found a taxi right outside the restaurant, headed for Lord & Taylor.

'Friday used to be the lightest shopping day midweek,' Claudia recalled as they settled themselves in the cab. 'Now – with the rash of discount coupons sent out regularly by the department stores - it's Mondays and Tuesdays that are light. The "no-coupon" days,' she joshed.

'I'll use your discount coupons to buy something for the kids,' Shirley said while they settled back in the taxi. 'I may not have a Lord & Taylor charge account – I wouldn't trust myself with one – but I do love your discount coupons.'

Claudia chuckled. 'I only shop on coupon days. I always feel as though I'm ahead of the game that way. Todd laughs at my little economies.'

'Bill and I do most of our shopping at the discount malls – and feel guilty about it.' Claudia lifted an eyebrow in question. 'I bitch because I'm working as a "temp" – when I get called – at twelve dollars an hour. These days the calls are sporadic. But those women – and it's mostly women – working in Wal-Mart and most discount places earn maybe seven dollars an hour. With no health insurance, no benefits. Twenty-two years ago we would have been among the protesters.' Shirley sighed. 'I guess I haven't got time in my life to protest any more. And that's sad—'

A few minutes past 4 p.m. Claudia dropped Shirley off to pick up her train home, then ordered the taxi driver to head south. It had been a good afternoon, she told herself. She always enjoyed spending time with the old college group. And since the move to New York, she and Shirley managed to see each other once a month and spoke on the phone almost daily. But no matter where Todd's job took them, she and Shirley kept in close contact.

Emerging from the cab in front of her condo, she was startled to see a red Jaguar parked a few spaces down. Todd drove a red Jaguar – but most of the time it was in the garage. Mildly curious, she sought the number on the license plate. Todd's car.

What was he doing home at this hour? Perhaps changing clothes for some business cocktail party, she surmised – which meant he wouldn't be home for dinner until very late or not at all. And he'd be too involved to call and tell her. But she should be used to that by now. The food she tossed away – when so many were starving in Third World countries!

She exchanged pleasantries with the doorman, took the elevator up to their penthouse apartment with its wraparound deck. She unlocked the door, walked inside – and froze. Three oversized valises sat in the foyer. She heard Todd talking to someone – on the phone, her mind pinpointed.

For no reason, she scolded herself, she felt a flutter of alarm. Where was Todd rushing with three oversized valises? Why wasn't he at the office?

'It's okay.' He was soothing someone now. 'We can deal with this. My passport is in order – we'll have no problems. Just wait there – I'll pick you up. We'll make the flight on time—'

'Todd—' Her voice sharper than she intended as she strode to the door of what had been Jill's bedroom and now was his. His words zigzagging across her mind. 'Todd, what's happening?'

'Hank's being indicted! He swore it couldn't happen. An hour ago they took him away in handcuffs!' Hank Reynolds was his boss. His face etched with panic, Todd tossed file folders into an attaché case. 'I'm cutting out! My passport's in order – it was renewed when we flew to London last spring—' He closed the attaché case, turned to her. 'I'll be next – if I stay around here.'

Claudia was bewildered. 'Why was Hank indicted? How does that affect you?'

'Damn it, you're always so stupid! He was indicted on fraud charges and racketeering. Don't you read the papers? Don't you know what's going on? We took some short cuts. We should have made millions – we could have returned the funds we borrowed—'

Borrowed?

'But some asshole blew the whistle. We tried to fix things – it didn't work. Now we're in deep shit. I'm not hanging around to be indicted.'

'Todd, I don't understand—' Her head was spinning. *This is unreal.*

'You've always lived in a dream world—' He glared at her in contempt. 'I have no time to waste here. We have to make a late-afternoon flight.'

'Who's we?' *Where is he going?*

He frowned impatiently. 'I'm flying to South America – with this woman who's going to back me in some business down there. She's got great connections.' He avoided Claudia's eyes. 'Her father's a judge. He'll arrange for a "quickie" divorce.'

He's divorcing me?

'I'll – be marrying her once the divorce comes through.'

'Where in South America?' *Does it matter?*

'It's better that you don't know,' he brushed this aside. 'In case you're questioned.'

I could be involved in this craziness?

'I've had enough of this rat race – it's time to make a fresh start.' He was checking the contents of a jacket pocket, blowing in relief as he studied his passport. 'I'll be in touch about the divorce papers – I'll write you care of Jill—'

'Why can't you write me here?' *None of this makes sense.*

He took a deep breath, exhaled. 'We've lost the condo.'

What does he mean?

'I borrowed to the hilt. The bank's taking over. You'll be served with eviction papers some time next week.'

Claudia stared at him in disbelief. 'How could we lose the condo?'

'Hank and I got in over our heads. We were fighting to save our hides—' He gestured. 'We couldn't.'

'How did we lose the condo?' she persisted. *We own jointly – I'd have to sign any loan papers.*

'I signed for you,' he yelled, then seemed cowed for a moment. 'I didn't want to worry you.'

That's a lie.

'Nothing can happen until Monday at the earliest – but clear out by then. Bring in some furniture buyer – unload everything.'

'What about our stock portfolio? The CDs?' *I must be out of the condo by Sunday night, he's saying. How can this be happening?*

'Nothing's left,' he broke in. Eyes evasive. 'Just whatever's in the checking account.'

He's cleaned out our stocks, the CDs, to bankroll the fresh start he talked about.

'Look, I can't waste time – I have a plane to catch.'

With some woman he's going to marry in South America.

'I'll take two of the valises down to the car, come back for the other.'

'What about the car?' she asked.

'I've made arrangements. It'll be shipped to South America.'

What about the bank loan? But I'm not on that – the bank can't come after me for payments. I'm not even on the car registration. Todd wanted it that way.

He brushed past her, strode down the hall to the foyer. She heard the door slam behind him.

Don't bother to lock – he's coming back for the other valise. Then out of my life. Twenty-two years together and it can end this way?

I won't fall apart – I have to handle this. Larry has two more years in college after this year – and I can't count on Todd for anything. How much can I expect from a furniture buyer? We spent a fortune – I'll get a pittance.

7

Where will I live? How will I find a job in this horrible job market? I've never worked in my life except summer jobs during college. How will I survive?

Two

Claudia sat on a corner of the living-room sofa and stared into the dwindling light of the early evening. Numb with shock. This was something that happened to other women. Other families. Jill and Larry would be so upset.

All at once the numbness evaporated. She had much to do. Call the kids tonight. They had to know what was happening. Let them take whatever they had stored here. First thing tomorrow morning she must call in a used-furniture dealer. She'd find a list in the classified phone directory.

She flipped on a lamp, reached for the phone, called the bank's 24-hour line to learn what remained in their checking account. She winced when the bank clerk reported a balance of $48.12. Shouldn't she have known Todd would strip the account?

All at once she remembered the diamond ring and the matching earrings that had been her Christmas present just before the New York move. They'd cost Todd a small fortune. They should bring a substantial chunk of cash. *Did Todd take them, too?*

She leaped to her feet, dashed to her bedroom, moved a print that hid the tiny wall safe. The safe was open – only papers relating to the condo purchase four years ago lay there. Hope collapsed – for a moment. Now – with a surge of relief – she remembered. She'd worn the ring and earrings two evenings ago – when she and Todd went to the dinner party at the Reynoldses' townhouse. She'd been tired – she hadn't bothered to put them back in the safe. She darted to her dressing table, pulled open a drawer. There they lay – shining up at her. Todd hadn't found them.

Todd told people who admired the ring and the matching earrings a fanciful story about how hard he'd worked to buy her a fine engagement ring – and how with his first major deal he'd bought her the earrings. He'd bought them to make an impression on his new associates. He knew there'd be much socializing among them.

The jewelry would bring a few thousand, she told herself – optimistic for the moment. Something to tide her over until she found a job. A job that would provide funds to see Larry through college?

Her heart began to pound as she considered job hunting. What could she do? In the college years she'd worked in a small boutique. No other work experience. She was computer literate because she helped Todd from time to time with correspondence, reports. But how would that fit into a resumé?

She'd graduated with a major in English and a minor in speech and drama. *What kind of job am I capable of holding? I raised two kids. I gave endless elaborate dinner parties. I managed a household. I did volunteer work.*

Exhausted, she stretched out on the king-sized bed and tried to clear her head. By Sunday evening she must be out of this condo or face the humiliation of eviction. Utilities had to be cancelled. She must pack up whatever she meant to take with her. She must find a place to live. *By Sunday night.*

She shuddered at the cost of spending even a few nights in a Manhattan hotel. She must find boxes for packing. She fought against panic as she considered finding storage space. For the moment she could store things in Shirley's basement, she told herself. Shirley would drive in with the car and help her.

At times like this, she thought wryly, it was good to have families. Todd had been estranged from his family since college graduation – a situation that had bewildered her. An only child, she'd lost both parents in a plane crash weeks after graduation.

She and Todd had been married in City Hall – with Shirley and Daisy as their witnesses. Jill and Larry never knew their grandparents. Never knew aunts or uncles because both her parents had been the only child in their families. But enough of this. Call Shirley.

She reached for the phone on her bedside table. She and Shirley were always there for each other in crisis moments. Her hand trembling, she punched in Shirley's phone number.

'Hello,' a bubbly young voice chirped.

'Hi, Annie—' Claudia strived to sound cheerful. 'This is Claudia. Is Mommie home?'

'She's in the kitchen making dinner,' Annie said. 'But she'll want to talk to you.'

Moments later Shirley was on the phone, listening – stunned – while Claudia briefed her on what was happening.

'You'll come out and stay with us until you can think things through,' Shirley said firmly. 'I'll drive in first thing in the morning and—' Then all at once she was silent.

'Shirley?'

'I just had a brainstorm.' Shirley's voice was electric. 'You know my sister Laura's flying out to Iraq on Sunday—'

'You couldn't persuade her not to go?' Claudia knew that Shirley was terrified of this TV assignment that Laura – her younger sister – had just wangled for herself.

'Oh, Laura's sure this is the chance of a lifetime. She can't wait to get over there. She's on a four-month contract – and I'll be a wreck for every day she's gone,' Shirley admitted. 'She'd love to sublet her apartment to you. She inherited it years ago – and it's rent stabilized. But she couldn't bring herself to have a stranger move in. It's only for four months,' Shirley cautioned, 'but it'll give you time to look around and find something.'

'That would be a godsend!' She'd been in Laura's apartment – in Manhattan's Gramercy Park area – last year, when they'd arranged a surprise birthday party for Shirley. The apartment was a tiny one bedroom, but it would be fine for her. And there was a convertible sofa – Larry could stay with her over the Thanksgiving and Christmas holidays.

'I'll call her right now—'

'I'm getting you at dinner time,' Claudia said in sudden awareness. 'Annie said you were cooking.'

'Dinner can wait another ten minutes. I'll call Laura and get right back to you.'

Minutes later Shirley was on the phone with Claudia again.

'It's a deal. I'm coming into town first thing in the morning. You'll have packing to do – stuff that needs to be stored in our basement.' Shirley echoed her thoughts. 'And we'll find time to go over and talk with Laura. She was in such a rush these past days she hadn't even arranged to turn off the electric and the phone and cable while she was gone – so you'll have services. I'll see you first thing in the morning,' Shirley reiterated. 'I'll tell Bill it's his day to handle the kids – I'll be in the city with you. But right now let me go feed the brood before they disown me. And you send out for dinner. I'm the one that needs to lose weight – you're perfect.'

It amazed Claudia to realize that she was hungry. She went out to the kitchen, found a salmon steak left over from last evening's dinner because Todd had – presumably – a dinner meeting with Hank. A baked potato would become home fries – in a non-stick pan requiring no oil or butter. Salad left over from last evening's dinner and sufficiently fresh for tonight.

She carried her dinner tray into the living room. The silence in the apartment was full of ominous undertones. In a sudden need to break the silence, she crossed to flip on the TV. She watched the national and world news without absorbing a word. Her mind in chaos.

In a few hours her whole life had been turned upside down. Tomorrow was a threatening obstacle course. Why couldn't she have seen what was happening with Todd? He'd been

11

irritable lately – but he was often irritable. Irascible, she taunted herself. He brought all his anger and frustration home to her. Long ago she'd learned to retreat into silence.

He never talked about business. But she read the newspapers, magazines, watched TV business programs. She knew about the Wall Street scandals that had been erupting over the past few years. Yet never had she suspected that Todd might be involved in something that would send him fleeing the country.

The kids had to be told what was happening. Oh God, what an awful thing to dump on them! Would there be ugly newspaper stories? Would she – and the kids – be questioned? She felt sick at the prospect.

Todd wasn't a partner in the company – though he had anticipated that would happen shortly. Was he running in panic after he saw Hank taken away in handcuffs? *Please God, let it be nothing more than that. Let the kids and me not be involved in this horror.*

Friday would be party night for college students, she surmised. Call Larry late. Very late. That went for Jill, too, she reminded herself. Jill's working hours were obscene. If she were to break down the hours she spent on the job, her fancy salary would not appear so fancy.

Claudia ate without tasting. Her mind charged ahead. For four months she had an apartment. She'd shop around in selling the jewelry – including her platinum and diamond wedding ring. She'd never wear it again. She wouldn't be destitute.

Maybe – just maybe – she'd come up with enough from the jewelry to see Larry through the balance of the school year. She'd manage to live on whatever the furniture brought. Shirley said she was to settle with Laura on the rent for the apartment when Laura returned from Iraq.

Take one day at a time, she exhorted herself. Right now the most important thing was to contact Larry and Jill. She abandoned the pretense of eating dinner, reached for the phone. She'd leave a message on Larry's answering machine: 'Call me, Larry – whatever time you get in. It's important.'

As she'd anticipated, Larry was not at the off-campus apartment he shared with two other students. She'd talk with him later. No classes tomorrow – he'd come into the city and clear out what he wished to keep from his room.

She debated a few moments about calling Jill at the office. No doubt in her mind that Jill would still be at work. Gearing herself for what must be done, she punched in Jill's private number, waited.

'Yes.' Impatience – annoyance – in Jill's voice.

'Jill, it's me,' she said. 'Whatever time you finish at the office, please come to the apartment. We need to talk.'

'Mom, it could be three a.m.,' she protested, but Claudia sensed her alarm at this call.

'Come here.' Claudia struggled for calm. 'I can't talk over the phone. Just come, darling—'

'Mom, are you okay?' Jill sounded frightened.

'I'm okay – but we have to make some adjustments in our lives. Whatever time you can get here will be fine. I'll be here.'

Three

In nightwear and slippers Claudia huddled in a corner of the sofa – one lamp providing muted illumination. Tense and cold despite the warmth of the apartment, she listened to Jill's shocked and indignant reaction to what had occurred in the past few hours. But she hadn't told Jill yet about the divorce – and the woman who was traveling with Todd to South America.

'How could he do this to you?' Jill raged. 'To lose the condo, walk out on you this way! How are you supposed to live?'

'I've got an apartment for the next four months.' She'd told Jill about Laura's taking off for Iraq. 'I'll find a job—'

She interpreted the dismay in Jill's eyes. *Where will Mom get a job? What can she do? She's a forty-three-year old woman with no business experience.* And this was a world where a woman – or man – over forty was too often considered 'over the hill' for anything but minimum-wage service jobs.

'I'll help as much as I can,' Jill began worriedly, 'but—'

'Darling, this is something I have to work out for myself.' *I don't expect the kids to support me. I'm still young. I've got to get out there and land a job.*

'I have an unexpected problem—' Jill gestured her frustration.

'What kind of problem?' Instantly her own situation retreated into the background. *Jill's leaving her systems analyst job? Where she was so confident she'd pass the two-year test and move up fast.*

'You know Sandy's kind of impetuous.' Jill's shrug was eloquent. Sandy was Jill's college roommate, shared her apartment now.

'What about Sandy?'

'She quit her job – she says she's had it with New York. She's applying for a job back home. At any rate she'll be moving out in a few days to return to Minneapolis. I'm stuck with paying thirty-four hundred a month!' For their East 60s two-bedroom luxury apartment with laundry rooms on every floor, stainless-steel kitchen with granite countertops, and rooftop health club. 'It's going to make an awful dent in my income.'

Claudia was startled. 'Have you any leads on a replacement for Sandy?' Jill and Sandy had been in their apartment barely five months. But she knew the few rental apartments in her building seemed to have transient tenants Four girls or guys – or a mixture – moved in, then one or two lost their jobs in this insane economy and zingo, the apartment was for rent again. At insane rentals. 'Somebody else from college?' *In the back of my mind I'd thought I could count on Jill to help with Larry's college tuition next year. Who expected this?*

'I don't know anybody who's looking – or willing to pay my kind of rent. Though it'll be furnished – that's a plus.'

'Sandy isn't selling her furniture?' Each had bought her own bedroom furniture, Claudia recalled. The living-room furniture had been contributed by the two sets of parents.

'Sandy put up a notice in the laundry room, but I doubt she'll get any calls.' Jill sighed. 'I shudder at the thought of sharing with a stranger.'

'You'll have to find someone to share – or live on an extremely tight budget.' A situation Jill had never encountered, Claudia thought with alarm. After rent and taxes Jill's impressive income would be minuscule.

'You could move in with me when Sandy leaves,' Jill offered. 'She'll—'

'I'm committed to a sublet for the next four months,' Claudia pointed out. *In a rent-stabilized apartment, thank God. When Boston dumped stabilization, Lois said, urban living was out of bounds for many local families.*

'Do you really have to be out of here by Sunday night?' Jill agonized. 'That sounds wild.'

'Dad said eviction notice could be served as early as Monday morning – by the marshal or whoever handles those things.' Claudia winced at the prospect of facing such a situation. *How can life change so drastically in a few hours?*

'Dad's a real bastard!' Jill slammed a fist on her knee in frustration.

'He's not the perfect husband and father.' Claudia's smile was sardonic. She took a deep breath. 'There's more. He's going to South America with some woman who – he says – will help set him up in business. He'll divorce me down there – he'll forward all the papers to you—'

15

'He's running off with that – that bimbo I saw him with last year!'

What is she talking about?

'I was in Boston – when my chess team was playing in a tournament there. He was staying at our hotel. He didn't see me – he was with this woman. All he could see was her—'

'Why didn't you tell me, Jill?' *How long had it been going on? How many other women when he was away on his business trips? And this explains Jill's coldness to her father in the last year.*

'I thought about it.' Jill was somber. 'I was so angry. And then I told myself maybe it was just a midlife crisis. I guess I was scared of how you'd react—'

'It's late and you must be exhausted,' Claudia began.

'I have to be at the office by nine tomorrow morning.'

Is any job worth the kind of hours she's putting in?

'I'll call the company car service – unless you want me to stay for the night?'

'No need, darling – call your car service. Shirley will be here first thing in the morning. She'll help with everything. But whatever you want that's stored here, arrange to take to your apartment by Sunday night.' All the silly little things the kids had saved through the years. Stuffed animals, paintings from art class, ice skates that hadn't been worn in years.

'Mom, you're going to be all right,' Jill said urgently. 'We'll see this through together.'

Claudia was dozing on the sofa when the phone rang. Instantly awake, she reached to respond – knowing it would be Larry.

'Hello, Larry?'

'Mom, are you okay?' His voice hoarse with fear.

'I'm all right. Your father's all right – that is, as far as his health goes—' Now, fighting for poise, she briefed Larry on what had happened in the past dozen hours – winding up with the divorce business.

'I don't believe this.' Larry sounded dazed. 'How could he

do this to you? What crazy stuff did he pull with the company?'

'I don't know the details. Just that Hank Reynolds was taken into police custody. Your father may be running in panic – we don't know how deeply he's involved. Dad's not a partner,' she emphasized. 'I gather he and Hank tried to buy their way out of this mess – but it wasn't working.'

'Jill's got a great job. I'll quit school. Between us we can—'

'You're not to drop out,' Claudia broke in. *How can I let that happen?* 'You'll complete this year somehow,' she insisted – with more bravado than conviction. 'Maybe you'll switch to state for next year. There are college loans—' Her voice ebbed away.

'I'll come into town tomorrow,' Larry began.

'Darling, be sure you have your keys. I'll be in and out during the day – taking care of what needs to be done. But we'll have dinner together at the apartment.'

'I'll be there in time for dinner,' Larry promised.

'We're going to be all right, Larry. We'll work things out.'

How do we work things out? I feel as though I'm in a sinking ship, out in the middle of the Atlantic.

Four

Claudia and Shirley sat at the breakfast table in the condo's eat-in kitchen and made a pretense of enjoying the omelet Shirley had made for them while Claudia had put up coffee and toast. The trauma of the past fifteen hours was etched on their faces. In the corner of the foyer were stacked the pile of shipping cartons Shirley had brought with her – raided from her basement, relics of endless household purchases through the years.

'Remember how I used to make my "everything" omelets on Sundays back in that creepy little apartment off campus?' Shirley's eyes were reminiscent.

'Those were good days,' Claudia said softly. The days you remembered forever.

'I can't believe we were ever so young, so carefree.' Shirley sighed. 'We were going to knock the world dead. I know to an awful lot of people Bill and I look as though we're living well. A nice house in suburbia – not a mansion on two acres but comfortable – two cars. To survive in suburbia two cars are a must. How else would we get around? But we still scrounge every month to pay the mortgage on the house and the car loans and try to bank a few bucks towards college – which gets higher every year.'

'We have to schedule today—' Claudia closed her eyes for an instant. 'I keep thinking, "This is a nightmare, and I'll wake up in a little while."'

'What about the utilities, the car loans – all that stuff?' Shirley asked in sudden alarm. 'Are the bills in Todd's name or yours?'

'Everything was in Todd's name. It was the macho thing with him.' Claudia was conscious of cynicism creeping into her voice. In earlier days she'd thought it was his way of saying he was taking care of his family. 'All the charge plates, all the household bills are in his name. The condo was bought jointly – because that was the accepted routine.'

'But that didn't stop Todd from forging your signature when he borrowed on the condo,' Shirley reminded. 'That isn't accepted routine.' *Insider trading wasn't accepted routine, either.*

'I must call Mattie,' Claudia realized. Mattie came in on Mondays and Thursdays to clean and was on duty to serve and clean up every time they entertained – which was often. She always handled the cooking herself – she found pleasure in providing perfect meals. 'I'll give her two weeks severance pay.' That was an obligation – Mattie had been with her almost three years. But that must be her last gesture of normal living.

18

'Maybe you ought to look at this as a change in career,' Shirley began.

'I've had no career,' Claudia dismissed this.

'Being a wife and mother is a career,' Shirley insisted. 'Women change careers in mid-life. You've always been into nutrition. What about a—?'

'No.' Claudia cut her off. 'I can't afford to go back to college – and where can you go in the nutrition field without a degree? I have to worry about paying rent and utilities and food bills.' Women – and men – did change careers in mid-life. There were stories in the newspapers about some dramatic switches. *But how can that happen for me? I have to worry about survival.*

'You have a list of used-furniture dealers?' Shirley brought Claudia back to the moment. 'You have such beautiful furniture. Perhaps you should keep a few special pieces – store them in our basement?' But Claudia was shaking her head decisively.

'I don't want anything from here to go with me – except my clothes and books and all the photo albums. I'm starting a new life – I don't need memories of the old.'

What did I do in the old life beside run the house? Shopping too much – out of boredom. Volunteer work along with 'the wives,' as Todd called them. That was the thing to do. A lot of reading and watching TV in the evenings because Todd was away so much. Cooking for the dinner parties was an escape. Something to be enjoyed.

'Okay, one more cup of coffee and let's take this show on the road.' Shirley strived for flippancy.

Claudia called the first name on her list of used-furniture dealers, explained that they'd sold their condo and must be out by Sunday evening.

'We've made a sudden decision to take a year's sabbatical in Europe,' she fabricated. 'We don't want to store the furniture – we prefer to sell and start afresh when we return.'

To her relief the dealer – no doubt impressed by their address, which indicated high-end furnishings – agreed to be over within an hour. If a deal was reached, he'd have trucks to pick up at the apartment by 4 p.m.

'Don't jump at the first offer,' Shirley warned, then laughed. 'I know, you can dicker with the best of them.'

Claudia grimaced in recall. 'All the moves we've made through the years, all the hiring.'

'Remember when you went with me to buy the Dodge suburban?' For an instant laughter lit Shirley's eyes. 'We talked with the salesman. You made the deal for me – because I'm always a nervous wreck in those situations. Then the manager came over to explain it was a big mistake – the Dodge would cost me another eleven hundred. You reached for your coat – with that look in your eye that said "I'm not taking this shit" – nodded to me to do the same. Right away the eleven hundred extra evaporated.'

'It was a routine act – only the gullible fall.' *But that isn't experience in the business world. What job skills do I have to offer?*

While they waited for the used-furniture dealer to arrive, Claudia and Shirley packed.

'I'll take the dishes, the pots, and the linens out to the house to store in the basement until you need them,' Shirley decreed.

'Let's leave that ghastly, ornate set of dishes Todd bought when we were in Germany last year. I'll use it over the weekend.' Again, Claudia was caught up in a sense of unreality.

'Laura's closet space isn't huge. She's storing clothes she's not taking with her in the hall closet, she said – you'll have the wall closet in the bedroom. That's not much,' Shirley worried.

'I'll mange,' Claudia broke in. 'I won't need the cocktail dresses, the formal gowns.' The heavy socializing belonged to a world now past – and not to be missed. 'Give them to that thrift shop your group runs. And I'll store the rest in your basement. Thank God, it's big.'

On schedule the used-furniture dealer arrived, and made an offer that was immediately rejected. Claudia forced herself to negotiate, arrived at a price shockingly low considering the original cost of their fine antiques, yet she sensed she would do little better elsewhere. And she had no time to play.

Every item of furniture with the exception of the beds and the dinette set in the kitchen was sold. At least, she realized belatedly, she and Larry wouldn't be sleeping on the floor in the sleeping bags, relics of the kids' camping trips. The breakfast table and chairs – rejected by the dealer – would be here for what meals would be had in the condo.

'Will you have a problem about the moving?' Shirley was solicitous. So many buildings refused to allow weekend movings.

'For once luck is on my side.' Claudia managed a twisted smile. 'The super is on a week's vacation. His replacement is – manageable.'

'How much will it cost you?'

'I'm sure a hundred will do it.' For a moment she was alarmed. Thank God, she always kept an 'emergency fund' hidden in her dressing table. There'd be five hundred in fifties there.

'Okay,' Shirley said, 'let's start loading my car.'

Aware of the 4 p.m. arrival of the pick-up trucks, Claudia and Shirley headed uptown for the meeting with Laura. Claudia noted that the building provided around-the-clock doormen. *Decent security.*

'The apartment below me was just rented for almost three times what I'm paying,' Laura reported. 'I can't figure out how the management gets away with it.'

Laura gave Claudia the pair of keys for the apartment and the mail box key.

'Pull out the utility bills – which will need to be paid,' Laura reminded, 'but just throw everything else – catalogues and ads, mostly – in the bottom of the hall closet. I'll be leaving for JFK at 2 p.m. – after that, the apartment is all yours for four months,' Laura effervesced.

Staying on schedule, Claudia and Shirley visited the jeweler.

'You have the bill of sale?' he asked.

Julie Ellis

'Right here—' With an impersonal smile Claudia reached into her Judith Lieber purse. The purchase price would mean nothing, she warned herself.

Again, minutes of dickering before a selling price was agreed upon. She'd be able to pay Larry's tuition for the next term, but he'd have to pick up a part-time job to handle his living expenses. She'd see him through till he found something, she vowed. Somehow, she'd manage that.

At 4 p.m. sharp the furniture dealer's men arrived. Claudia insisted everything was under control – Shirley was to go back home.

'Bill's had the kids all day,' she said tenderly. 'Go home and make dinner for them.'

Fighting for poise, Claudia watched while the furniture men crated and moved every item. No problem with the super's replacement. With the last crate being carried into the service elevator – Claudia watching from the condo door, Larry arrived.

He hurried from the elevator to her side, kissed her.

'You're okay, Mom?' His eyes pleaded for reassurance.

'I'm okay.' She forced a smile, nodded in the direction of the service elevator. 'There goes the furniture – except what they didn't want to take.' Collected lovingly – piece by piece – through the years, expected to last a lifetime.

Larry held her close – as though to protect her against the world while together they watched the service elevator door close on the last crate

'Dad's such a bastard!' Larry said with fresh rage. 'I never want to see him again!'

'I doubt that you will,' Claudia said drily while they walked together into the near-empty apartment. Larry sneezed three times. 'God bless you,' Claudia said automatically and was all at once fearful. *He isn't coming down with something, is he? Is our health insurance still in effect? When do we lose it? I can't afford health insurance for us on my own! Dear God, let us both stay healthy.*

'We'll go out for an early dinner,' Larry decided with an unfamiliar air of authority. 'Somewhere nice.' Taking over his father's role in their lives, Claudia thought with a rush of tenderness. He grinned. 'Jack just paid me back the hundred I loaned him at the beginning of the semester.' Jack was one of his two apartment-sharers. 'He's working weekends at a bar in town. He's going to talk to the owner about taking me on.'

'The owner won't have to worry about you drinking up the profits.' Claudia sought for an air of lightness. 'Not when you're allergic to alcohol.'

'Yeah – that's a plus.' He flinched as he glanced about at the emptiness of the foyer and the living room. 'Where shall we have dinner?'

'Let's have it here,' Claudia said gently. 'Scrounge to see what's in the fridge.'

'Whatever you say, Mom.'

He's treating me like a delicate flower. I'm not fragile – I can survive without Todd.

Together they explored the contents of the refrigerator, the freezer.

'What about spaghetti with grilled chicken strips?' she asked. 'With a big salad.' The crisper was loaded with salad makings. 'It'll be very fast and simple. For dessert hot apple slices topped with yogurt. Low-fat Cherry Garcia—'

'Yeah, the perfect balanced meal,' he teased. 'Protein, veggies, fruit.'

'You set the table—' She opened a cabinet door, pointed to the dishes. 'I'll cook.'

She had never felt closer to Larry than now, she thought with a surge of love as they went about their respective tasks. This was an awful blow to him. Seeing his home disappearing – literally – before his eyes. Knowing it was unlikely he'd be able to continue at his expensive college, would leave friends behind. But he was young and bright – and he'd do well at a state college. *We'll be able to handle that between us, won't we?*

'You'll come to me for Thanksgiving and Christmas,' she told him in a sudden need to reassure him that their lives would not be totally disrupted. 'I'll be living in Shirley's sister's

23

apartment,' she reminded him. 'It's small – but she has a convertible sofa in the living room. Shirley says it's fairly comfortable. And there's a health club on the roof if you're in the mood—'

'Dad cleaned out everything?' Larry's eyes searched hers.

'Everything—' She contrived a shaky smile. 'Except for my diamond ring and earrings. I hadn't put them in the bedroom safe as usual—'

'He was never much of a father,' Larry said with brutal candor. 'Except when he felt like playing the role.'

'He became a stranger in these past few years.' *The kids felt that, too. Why didn't I realize that?* 'The man I married disappeared.'

'Are you getting rid of these dishes?' All at once Larry seemed anxious to shift the conversation in a less personal direction. 'I've always hated them.'

'I never liked them, either,' Claudia confessed. Todd had bought them. They'd cost a fortune. One of the handy men might take them home. 'But we'll have to eat on them tonight.'

They focused on preparing dinner. Larry put up coffee, then remembered the radio in his bedroom, brought it into the kitchen to provide dinner music.

'Shirley brought a lot of cartons,' Claudia told him while they sat down to eat. 'I left some in your room – to pack what you'd like to take with you.'

'My books, CDs – all that crap.' Larry shrugged. 'I'll take care of it in the morning.'

Over dinner Larry talked about campus activities. He seemed confident about a weekend job. His roommates both worked – it wasn't a fate worse than death, Claudia consoled herself. For Todd it had been a source of pride that Larry could avoid that. She'd thought it was because he was eager to be a good provider for his family. It was a boost to his ego.

Larry's going to miss his friends. You get so close to room-mates in the first year or two away at school. But he survived all the moves through the years. He'll be all right.

They lingered over coffee – reminiscing about holidays through the years. Both reluctant to face the emptiness of the living room.

'Why don't we live dangerously and finish up that pint of Cherry Garcia?' Larry challenged with the charismatic smile so like her own. 'It's the low-fat,' he reminded.

'We'll do it. You bring it out,' Claudia ordered. 'I'm too stuffed to move.' *Is this the way people grow obese? They eat in hurt moments – or seeking momentary pleasure in the midst of desolation?*

Later – with the Cherry Garcia demolished and the dishes piled into the dishwasher, Larry glanced at his watch.

'The Sunday *Times* ought to be on sale at that newsstand around the corner, shouldn't it?'

'Most Saturday nights it's there about now,' Claudia recalled.

'I'll run down and pick it up,' Larry decided. Their flat-screen television set was gone. Only Larry's bedroom radio was available for diversion. Unexpectedly he smiled. 'It'll be like when we first moved to New York. We'd sit down on Saturday nights and read the Sunday *Times*.'

Those first weeks – before Larry made friends in his new school. Before Todd dragged me into the heavy socializing with his new business peers.

Larry went down to pick up the *Times*. Claudia changed from pantsuit to robe, replaced her low-heeled pumps – because she refused to wear high heels – for slippers. They'd read the *Times* here in the kitchen. Along with the furniture, the living room was devoid of lamps. She'd arranged for bedside lamps to remain in her bedroom and Larry's.

Larry returned with a report that the temperature was dropping. 'For late October, it's cold.' He dropped the newspaper on the table. 'Fat paper – a lot of ads,' he surmised.

'I'll put up more coffee,' Claudia said. 'That'll warm you up.' *Why does an empty apartment feel colder than normal? Because it hinted at empty lives?*

'I'll put it up,' Larry said. 'Decaf – or we'll never fall asleep tonight.'

'Right,' Claudia agreed. *How will I sleep tonight? My last night in this apartment.*

They sprawled in the comfortable captain's chairs that surrounded the table and focused on reading the newspaper. At intervals each made comments. Then all at once – cruising through the Sunday ads – Claudia felt a sudden excitement.

Miller's Manhattan – a high-end department store – ran two full-page ads – as usual. At the bottom of the second page a brief note reported that personnel was hiring sales associates for the approaching holiday season. Translated, sales associates meant salespeople. *I can do that.*

I'll lie about my experience in the boutique back in college days, move the time up. The boutique is closed – if anybody bothers to check. I'll be there at Miller's first thing Monday morning. I'll apply for a job. I can be a sales associate. Can't I?

Five

Claudia sat with Jill in the cozy neighborhood restaurant Laura had recommended – lingering over a late-evening snack. Larry had headed back for college three hours ago. She felt a towering love for her children – so warm and protective towards her when their own lives were being turned upside down. Jill might be out on her own now – but until this weekend she knew home was an ever-present refuge. And since Friday evening Larry knew an uncertain future lay ahead.

'Shall we have more coffee?' Jill was striving for a casual tone – as though this was an ordinary occasion.

'No more,' Claudia said tenderly. 'Go home, get to bed. You'll have another crazy work week ahead.'

'You're serious about applying for a job at Miller's tomorrow?' Jill seemed anxious. 'Maybe you ought to give yourself a week to—'

'Tomorrow,' Claudia brushed this aside. 'Considering the economy the employment office will probably be flooded. I want to go through my wardrobe, decide what to wear. Whatever – after my hasty packing it'll need to be pressed.' No calling for a pick-up from the neighborhood dry-cleaner. She hadn't ironed since the kids were small and Todd's salary at the bottom of the barrel. But other women pressed. Other women held jobs – and raised kids at the same time. For a lot of years she'd been spoiled.

'I'll go back to the apartment with you,' Jill said, reaching for the check.

'No, darling – you go on home.' *The kids are so sweet, so worried about me. I mustn't let them know how scared I am. Everybody knows that in divorce cases the wife almost always faces a painful drop in lifestyle. But I can deal.*

Claudia waited with Jill outside the restaurant until an empty taxi slid to a stop at the curb at a signal from Jill, then headed for her new apartment. She'd go to bed early tonight, she promised herself while she unlocked the door. She'd be applying for a job tomorrow morning. She mustn't look exhausted. Not forty-three years old and exhausted.

After a restless first night in Laura's apartment, Claudia awoke with a disconcerting suddenness. Instantly wide awake. The recall of the last sixty hours an unnerving assault. It wasn't a nightmare – it was reality. *This is the first day of my new life.*

She glanced about the unfamiliar bedroom, fought against a sense of claustrophobia at its small dimensions. Their first apartment – twenty-two years ago – had been a studio. Only when Todd moved into investment banking – and his salary began to rise – were they able to move into an apartment about the size of this.

By the time Larry was born, Todd was already talking

about their buying a house. In truth, nothing had been fine enough for Todd. Their elegant penthouse condo had paled before Hank's eighteen-room townhouse. What insanity had Hank and Todd committed that had landed Hank in jail and sent Todd running from the country? Or would he have run anyway, she taunted herself – to that woman he planned to marry?

Now an awareness of the day's objective rode over her. The urgency of finding a job – no matter how modest. Her heart pounding, she tried to envision what lay ahead. Would there be hordes of people in response to the ad? The jobless rate – especially in New York City – was unnerving.

She wouldn't be expected to bring a resumé, would she? No, she comforted herself. Applicants would fill out a form, be interviewed. And if she wasn't hired by Miller's it wouldn't be a disaster. Other department stores would be taking on holiday help.

Stay cool. The salaries are small – they won't be expecting an MBA. I can handle this.

She turned to the small, hand-painted clock on the night table – brought from the condo. It was minutes before 7 a.m. The Miller's employment office wouldn't open until ten. The intervening three hours an obstacle course she must face.

Early morning sunlight crept into the room despite the drawn drapes. She reached to flip on the bedside radio, found WQXR, waited for the weather report. It was 59 degrees, with a high of 64 projected.

She left the bed, showered, ordered herself to eat break-fast. Yesterday afternoon she'd shopped at the supermarket on Third Avenue, with Larry carrying the bags home for her. He'd been so solicitous about her having a loaded refriger-ator. Yesterday afternoon he'd brought over the stationary bike that had been part of their lives since the kids' pre-school days. Todd had belonged to a health club. She'd used the bike.

Devoid of appetite, she forced herself to down fruit juice,

scrambled eggs, wholewheat toast. Decaf coffee bubbled in Laura's coffee maker. She'd taught the kids from an early age about the importance of nutrition. In light moments they'd teased her about this:

'Mom, why didn't you take a master's in nutrition, build yourself a career? You're missing your vocation.'

There'd been no room in her life for going back to school. No room in her life for a career. Her career was being wife and mother. Was that a mistake? All the articles through the years about women 'having it all' hadn't disturbed her. Being Todd's wife, managing the household, catering to his entertainment needs, being a mother had been her career.

Shirley went back to work once Scott and Annie were in school full-time. Daisy had managed a career and motherhood – though she admitted her own mother took on much of the responsibility of raising her daughter. Beth and Bob had no children. How would Beth have handled the situation? Lois – with four kids – never considered a career.

She lingered over a second cup of coffee, then rinsed her breakfast dishes and loaded them into the dishwasher. The block of time to fill before she could approach Miller's employment office loomed over her like an ominous dark cloud.

All right, get dressed. Wear the black Givenchy pantsuit she'd pressed last night. One silver chain. Her black Coach purse. Ferragamo pumps.

The phone rang, startled her. She reached for the cordless in its kitchen niche.

'Hello.'

'How're you doing?' Shirley's voice, buoyant yet compassionate.

'I'm surviving.' A shaky defiance in her own voice. 'I'm assuming the employment office doesn't open until 10 a.m. – when the store opens.'

'Don't sound as though you'll be heading for the guillotine,' Shirley scolded. 'And don't be upset if you're not hired. All the department stores will be hiring Christmas help. You'll land in one. And as efficient as you are,' she predicted, 'you'll be held on after the holidays.'

'Efficient?' Claudia was startled. *I was a stay-at-home mom – whose kids have flown the coop. What's efficient about that?* 'You're out of your mind—'

'Every time you and Todd made a move to another state, you handled every detail – he never lifted a finger,' Shirley recalled. 'Every household crisis you handled. That dreadful fire in the Beverly Hills house the very day you moved in – when the slimy insurance people tried to claim you weren't covered. Who went to court to fight them? Todd was always too busy. Bill always said you're the smartest business woman he's ever encountered.'

'Let's hope somebody believes I'll make a satisfactory sales associate.' *Bill – and Shirley – see me as efficient?*

They talked another few minutes, until a looming battle between Scott and Annie demanded Shirley's intervention. Claudia glanced at her watch. A long wait before it would be time to leave for Miller's employment office. Meanwhile, dress, check make-up.

I'll walk. I can make it in thirty-five minutes. I won't have to ride the bike tonight. And I'll save – how much is a bus fare in New York these days?

Claudia was relieved to see only about a dozen women – and one man – sitting in the reception area of Miller's employment office. Considering the unemployment situation, she'd expected a mob scene. Of varying ages, they all were absorbed in filling out what Claudia assumed were application forms.

The woman behind the desk at one side of the room smiled at Claudia, beckoned to her.

'Just sign your name here.' She pointed to the clipboard at a corner of her desk. 'And fill out this application.' She extended one to Claudia. 'You'll be called in the order of your arrival.'

'Thank you.' Claudia accepted the form, retreated to one of

the few vacant chairs located about the room. She'd walked around the block three times in an effort to bolster her confidence. Still, it was only ten minutes past 10 a.m.

Reaching into her purse for a pen, she was conscious of covert glances from several of the other women. Two were at least a dozen years older than herself, she surmised. And employers were forbidden to ask for ages. Of course, she reminded herself, that could be deduced from information elicited on the application forms.

The door swung open. A casually dressed man with a sheaf of folders under one arm strode into the room. Not tall but with a carriage that gave him a semblance of height. A charismatic yet impersonal smile. With a casual glance about the occupants, a nod for the woman at the desk, he disappeared down the hall from the reception area.

'Isn't he cute?' the heavily made-up twenty-something who sat beside Claudia murmured to the twenty-something beside her.

'Yeah, for an older man. That's Michael Walsh – the guy brought into the store a little while ago to create some magic.' She giggled. 'My sister works here part-time. She says he pokes his nose into everything. The rumor is that the main office out in Chicago is threatening to close this store unless the sales figures jump up a lot.'

'But not before Christmas?' The other twenty-something was alarmed.

'Probably the Christmas sales will tell the tale.' She shrugged. 'It all depends on what Wonder Boy pulls off.'

Michael Walsh paused before going into his own office, backtracked to the woman assigned to interviewing applicants for sales associate positions.

'The woman in the black pantsuit,' he told her. 'Hire her.'

'After her interview?' A hint of sarcasm in her voice.

'Put her through the regular routine – but hire her.' Faintly sharp now. *I know the top echelon hates me – I'm the outsider here to show them their mistakes. But I'd thought further down the line I was accepted.* 'That woman has class. She'll do well.'

'Right, Mr Walsh.' She retreated, as though sensing she might have overstepped acceptable boundaries.

He settled himself in his office, checked meetings scheduled through the day. The woman in the black pantsuit lingered in his mind. There was a quiet authority about her, just in the way she sat there in the reception area.

Probably she'd been dumped from some well-paying position – in favor of someone not long out of college and willing to work for half her salary. Some job that was not exportable, he thought with black humor. She was over-qualified for the job here – but her financial situation required an income. Even an income far below what was normal for her.

He'd encountered some resentment from the executive level at his insistence on thorough training of every sales associate. Let them learn to be polite, helpful, courteous. Charge account customers to be addressed by name.

He'd checked around during his first weeks in the area. Manhattan was little different from White Plains. The smart stores understood they must cater to customers in the present world. Those were the stores that would survive.

Dolores – his very protective secretary – knocked lightly and walked into the office.

'You have a meeting in fifteen minutes,' she reminded. 'Shall I have coffee sent up from the restaurant?'

'For three,' he approved. 'They're not going to be happy at what I have to tell them.' He'd dug up substantial indications that the two were taking kickbacks from suppliers.

His eyes settled on his desk calendar. He froze. *Damn, I should have mailed out Lisa's check this morning – to make sure it arrives in Scottsdale before the first of the month. She throws a fit if she's a day late in the mortgage payments on her condo.*

He knew that some of his top-earning associates here in the store made snide remarks behind his back about his spartan lifestyle – despite his substantial income. They didn't know he was in bondage to his ex-wife. He was forty-two years old, he jeered at himself, and all he saw ahead was another twenty-three years in a job that gave him only a small satisfaction. But an urgently needed paycheck.

His mind traveled to the elegant woman in the expensive black pantsuit who sat waiting to be interviewed. Life had not been kind to her, either, he suspected.

Six

Claudia waited in an aura of disbelief for the 'down' elevator to arrive. She was hired. She was a trainee sales associate at Miller's Manhattan. The final conversation with her interviewer ricocheted in her mind:

'Normally we would have you start next Monday, but an order just came through to enlarge our sales staff immediately. We'd like you to come in tomorrow morning – 9 a.m. sharp – to undergo one-on-one orientation. You'll begin work on Wednesday morning. You'll receive all necessary instructions during the orientation period.'

She'd passed the age barrier. A small miracle in the current era. What about the two older women who'd been waiting to be interviewed along with her? Had they made it?

Now reality moved in. How demanding could Miller's be, considering the salary they offered?

A chill shot through her. Even before taxes she'd be earning little more than the cost of her rent – in a rent-stabilized apartment. Which was hers for just four months. She shuddered at the prospect of paying current market rates. But don't think ahead – take one day at a time. That was the road to survival.

The elevator slid to a stop. She rode down with a pair of

stockmen – one gloating about the amount of overtime he was piling up.

'Man, that don't mean good for me,' the other complained. 'It messes up my second-job schedule.'

Claudia absorbed what was being said. All right, she'd look for ways to add a second job. Weren't statistics always being spouted about how many Americans were working two and three jobs? Look around, focus on what else she could do. Still, it was a morale booster to know she'd acquired a job on the first try.

She left the store, headed south in the brilliant sunlight. She'd walk home – it was good exercise, she told herself. And kind on her budget. Now she felt a glimmer of hope for tomorrow. So the job was temporary – it was hers until the end of the year.

Back in the apartment she called Shirley.

'I got the job,' she reported jubilantly. 'I start tomorrow.'

'That's great.' Shirley sounded relieved.

'The salary's small,' she admitted.

'It'll be smaller after taxes come out,' Shirley warned.

'How much smaller?' *Todd was always screaming about high taxes – but he was making a lot of money.*

'Listen to Mommie,' Shirley ordered and provided a likely breakdown. 'If Larry is working, I'm not sure you'll be able to take him off as a dependent—'

Claudia groaned. 'After withholding, my paycheck will just about pay my rent and utilities.' She flinched as she considered this. 'No way can I buy health insurance for Larry and me.' *What do people do if somebody in the family gets sick and they have no insurance? If they're working – even at low-wage jobs – they're ineligible for Medicaid.*

'What about the job?' Shirley was solicitous. 'No health insurance?'

'It's temporary – no health insurance. Of course, I can buy anything in the store at a twenty per cent discount.' Ironic humor colored her voice for an instant. *How much spending can a sales associate afford? Unless she lives at home and pays nothing into the household.*

'Claudia, health insurance is urgent.' Shirley was alarmed. 'I know neither you nor Larry may ever need it, but—' Her voice ebbed away.

'I'll worry about that later. I'll get a second job. People do that these days.' Defiance blended with anxiety. 'Meanwhile, let's be positive. Larry and I must remain healthy.'

What other potential catastrophe have I overlooked?

Michael glanced at his watch. It was past 8 p.m. This was a night when the store closed for business at 7 p.m. After Thanksgiving they'd begin the longer holiday hours. *Go home – you've been here a dozen hours.*

He threw papers into his briefcase – because inevitably he'd want to study figures before going to sleep - then headed through the night-darkened floor to the elevators. He was conscious of hunger – he'd been too busy up till now to think about food. Dinner would wait until he arrived home. Restaurants had no place in his personal budget.

He found an odd relaxation in cooking, with classical music from his stereo filling the air. An hour away from the demanding business world. His cherished escape hatch.

Out of the store, he relished the night air – refreshing, invigorating. A taxi slowed down, as though the driver anticipated a fare. No, that was a luxury he couldn't afford. Head for the subway.

On the train headed north he considered his situation. If he succeeded in pulling the Manhattan store out of the red, he'd see a substantial raise in salary. A healthy bonus. His lifestyle could improve. Lisa couldn't increase her demands.

How had he got himself into his insane situation? His mind filtered back through the years. The only bright spot the twenty-seven months after college that he'd spent with the Peace Corps in Africa. Mom and Dad would have been so proud of him. They'd come to parenthood late, rejoiced in having a child.

Just before he'd left college his father had died, and three months later his mother. They hadn't been old – both in their early sixties, he remembered with fresh pain. Later, at loose ends – with a small inheritance – he'd gone back to school for an MBA. And that's when he met Lisa – a clerk in the Admittance Office.

She was sweet and appealing – in those first months. And he was hurting. Not till later – when they were married – had he realized she expected his MBA to be a path to riches.

When she discovered she was pregnant, he was elated. They'd be a family now, he'd told himself. But she didn't want the baby. Even now – all these years later – he could hear her voice:

'*You knew I didn't want to have a baby.*' She'd never said a word about that. '*You plotted it deliberately! You wanted your damn family!*' On several occasions she'd forgotten her birth-control pills.

The baby – his precious daughter – died within minutes of birth. Lisa went through two operations. She complained of constant pain, became a semi-invalid. He dreaded coming home each night.

In the first couple of years the White Plains store had been his escape from Lisa and her endless complaints. About their income – comfortable when she'd envisioned a luxurious lifestyle. About the state of her health – which she blamed on him.

Three doctors – after endless tests – had labeled her symptoms psychosomatic. She'd been outraged, clung to her invalid status. A fourth – a psychiatrist – suggested she try a change of scenery. She'd decided Scottsdale, Arizona would be the perfect refuge for her. Expensive Scottsdale.

'*The weather will be good for me – and the Mayo Clinic is there.*' But she lost her health insurance once they were divorced – and who would offer health insurance to someone in her condition? He paid endless medical bills. Part of the atrocious divorce settlement.

Lisa knew that he couldn't gamble on quitting his job at Miller's White Plains to go with her to Scottsdale – that was security for both of them. That was when she offered him a divorce. With non-negotiable stipulations.

She'd demanded a condo and a live-in attendant to care for her, along with routine living expenses – to rise with inflation. With his steady promotions and rising income, he figured he could handle this if he endured drastic budgeting. And it was a blessed escape.

Lisa moved to Arizona, divorced him. After the first year in Scottsdale she concluded no doctor could help her. She'd remain in precarious health.

He hadn't seen her in all these years. Their only contact the monthly checks he mailed to her. If he was a day late, he'd receive an irate phone call.

The train pulled into the West 72nd Street station. Michael strode onto the platform and up the stairs into the night. Belatedly he plotted his dinner. In those early days – back from the Peace Corps assignment – he'd thought longingly about going into the restaurant business. Gourmet food, he'd told himself, that met high nutrition standards. It was a market whose time had come. But where was he to find a backer? This was far beyond what Mom and Dad could have provided.

Mom and Dad had urged him to go back to school for his MBA. Dad – who'd spent his working life as a member of an accounting firm – worried about his fascination with the restaurant field.

'Michael, the restaurant business – even if you could find backing – is a huge gamble. Get your MBA – it's like a trust fund.'

He strode along the night street without seeing – impatient to be within the private confines of his small apartment. Here was a treasured oasis of solitude. Flip on the radio to WQXR for whatever classical masterpieces they offered for his dinner hour. Try to brush from his mind the relentless challenge of bringing Miller's Manhattan out of the red.

He forced himself to consider dinner preparations. He'd brought a salmon steak down from the freezer to defrost. The baby spinach would be quick – he had slivered almonds in the fridge to add to it. The Yukon Gold baked potato left over

37

from last night would become home fries in a pan that required little oil.

In his tiny Manhattan kitchen he set about preparing his dinner to a background of Beethoven's 'Moonlight Sonata.' His mind flashed back to this morning. To the lovely, elegant woman in the smart black suit who sat in the employment office in response to the store's ad for holiday help.

He'd issued instructions to hire her. He'd see her again. *But why am I thinking about her? Why am I feeling this way? There's no room in my life for a woman. I'm in bondage.*

Seven

Claudia awoke before the alarm went off. She heard the sound of rain pounding against the windows like an ominous symphony. This would be a slow day at the store, she guessed. Women – and most of Miller's customers were women – would wait for a more pleasant day to shop.

She gazed up at the ceiling with a sense of amazement. She'd been working at Miller's for two weeks and two days – and she'd made no terrible blunders, as she'd feared at inter-vals. Fran Golden – the friendly, late-forties sales associate in her department – had sensed her insecurity, had assured her she'd handle herself well.

'Just looking at you I knew that. I've been here seventeen years – and I've seen them come and go. The money is shitty, sure – but the checks are there every week. I bake cakes for a circle of steady customers – that adds to my income. But I just hope Michael Walsh puts the store on a profitable basis. I don't want to have to go looking in this rotten job market.'

Fran said Michael Walsh had started the one-on-one

orientation, had hammered the need to be courteous, helpful, and never impatient – no matter what the customer demanded. *He's one of those high-powered executives who burst into a store like a tornado, lay down rules, dump anybody who can't comply – and move on to the next trouble spot.*

Still, Fran said most of the sales and stockroom staff thought he was great – except for the handful he'd fired. She said, too, that he was having battles with the executive staff. *They resent him – he's in too big a rush to turn the store around to worry about diplomacy.*

The shriek of the alarm clock punctured her introspection. Time to get up, dress, have breakfast. She suspected this would be a day of steady rain. Today she'd take a bus uptown rather than walk – though she deplored the need to spend the bus fare.

Four dollars a day, twenty dollars a week leaves a big hole in a small salary check. Isn't there some saving with a metro card for bad days? I'll have to look into that. Wear rainboots today – no need to spoil my Ferragamo pumps.

She'd put herself on a tight budget. The money from the furniture and the jewelry must remain intact to see Larry through this school year. In the summer they'd worry about how to finance his junior year – away from the spiraling Ivy League fees.

Still, it was unnerving to see her spendable cash evaporate in the course of each week – with no emergency reserve. She remembered how Shirley sought out supermarket sales, cut coupons from fliers. And Fran, too, shopped for food with an eye on the sales items. It was a whole new way of life – but didn't most people in this world live that way?

Under the stinging hot shower she thought about her conversation last evening with Jill. Each day – nervous about what they might find – Jill and Larry searched the *New York Times* for news of Hank Reynolds. She refused to spend a dollar for a daily newspaper – not in her budget.

'Hank Reynolds is fading into the woodwork. Not a word anymore. He'll wiggle out,' Jill predicted. 'His wife is loaded

– she'll come across with money to save herself from scandal.'
Up till now Todd had talked with scorn about Mrs Reynolds'
tightness with money.

It was so sweet, the way Jill and Larry made a point of
calling her almost every day. And, thank God, the three of
them were beginning to feel less fearful of being dragged into
Todd's shady activities. For his own reasons, she surmised,
Hank was not implicating Todd – as Todd had feared. The
family was in the clear.

Claudia was dawdling over a second cup of decaf in the
living room when the phone rang. Shirley, she guessed with
a warm smile and picked up.

'Hello.'

'This is a rotten day to go to work,' Shirley commiserated.

'Hey, in this job market I'm lucky to have a job to go to.'

'Have you seen this morning's *Times*?'

'That's a luxury I forego.' But her heart began to pound. At
regular intervals she'd had frightening visions of a squad of
detectives invading the apartment, shooting questions at her.
'What am I missing?'

'Hank Reynolds hit the financial pages this morning,' Shirley
reported. 'He's changed lawyers. It appears he's about to make
a deal. If it was a woman,' she drawled, 'they'd be hounding
her into the ground.'

'That would mean Todd is off the hook.' She was conscious
of a shaky relief. 'For the kids' sake I hope it's true.'

'How's the job?'

'I'm hanging in there. I haven't worn a pair of heels since
the first day.' Claudia chuckled, remembered the state of her
feet at the end of that first day. 'I'm in my low-heeled pumps
and sedate pantsuits. Oh, I took your advice – I brown-bag
my lunch. The restaurants are a madhouse from twelve to one,
when I go to lunch.' She shuddered, recalling the lunchtime
scene. 'It's a big saving, too. And I'm not alone in this.'

Fran was candid. Lunch was yogurt most days. *'Once a
week I splurge – I have a grilled-chicken sandwich from one
of the fast-food joints.'*

In a corner of her mind Claudia recalled that someone on the floor had said that Michael Walsh was too busy to lunch at either of the restaurants in the store. *'Can you believe it? A guy like that brings his lunch from home every day.'*

'Claudia, I have to run. Annie's home with a cold – you know, demands every minute. I'll call you tonight.'

'Poor baby, I hope she feels better soon. Talk to you later.'

Michael Walsh was the man who'd walked through the reception room of the employment office the day she'd applied for the job. There was something commanding – almost charismatic – about him, she recalled. She remembered the comments of the two twenty-somethings who'd sat beside her.

'Isn't he cute?' 'Yeah, for an older man. My sister works here part-time. She says he pokes his nose into everything.'

He was probably the chain's top-drawer troubleshooter, going from one store to another. But it would be awful for Fran if the store closed. How long had she been working at Miller's? Seventeen years. *I was working as a wife for twenty-two years – and then one day I was fired.*

She didn't want to think beyond the Christmas season – when she'd be out there looking again for a job. She thrust to the back of her mind the reminder that she had an apartment for less than four months now. And nobody expected a drastic drop in rentals.

By the time she left for the store, the rain had become a steady downpour. Dreary and discomforting. She carried her shoes in a tote, was pleased that she'd decided to wear a lightweight raincoat over her suit. Was it her imagination, or were dry-cleaning prices soaring? Fran said she bought nothing that wasn't washable except for wool slacks.

An unoccupied taxi cruised into view. She fought an urge to lift an arm to summon the driver. *No. Not in my budget. Take the Third Avenue bus.*

Traffic was moving slowly this morning. It seemed forever before she boarded a bus. But she had a seat, she comforted herself. The hems of her slacks were damp from the rain. Her wet umbrella pressed into the tiny space allotted each

41

passenger. Still, she didn't have to push her way into a packed, smelly subway car.

Fran was already on the floor when she emerged from the morning ritual at her locker.

'What a shitty day,' Fran greeted her. 'Not even this morning's ad in the *Times* will bring out customers. And a slow day never seems to end. I'd much rather be busy.'

'The sweater table over there needs some straightening up,' Claudia decided.

'Okay, we'll make work.' Fran was philosophical. She uttered a faint, disparaging sound. 'Look what's coming. The diaper brigade.'

Claudia's gaze followed Fran's. Two young men she recognized as being part of the display department were dragging cardboard cut-outs from the elevator. Life-size models wearing clothes from the company's own line.

'They love to sell their own line,' Fran drawled while she and Claudia rearranged a sweater table and the display pair argued about the best locale for the cut-outs. 'The profits go way up. Everything's made in Indonesia or China or someplace where labor is paid twenty-two cents an hour – and there's no middle man.'

Claudia shuddered. 'It's scary, the way the country's losing jobs.' She remembered what Lou Dobbs had said on CNN last evening. Not just manufacturing jobs were being exported. Now it was clerical and well-paying professional jobs, as well.

'Every one of those cut-out models looks about sixteen,' Fran complained.

'I heard a woman in the ladies' lounge say there's going to be informal modeling in the restaurants starting tomorrow,' Claudia recalled. 'Live models.'

'The store does that every once in a while,' Fran said. 'I can't afford to eat in their fancy restaurants – but if I could those high fashion models would make me feel I should stop eating for a month.' She sighed. 'I'm always going to start dieting next week.'

'Those six-foot, anorexic, twenty-year-old models can be

intimidating. Why can't they use trim, attractive 40-ish models that customers can identify with? Can't they understand that Miss Anorexia of 2004 is a put-off?'

'Whoops!' Fran grimaced. Her eyes eloquent.

Claudia followed her gaze. Michael Walsh – surrounded by a cluster of display department people – was scarcely four feet away. He'd stopped dead, was staring hard at her.

He heard me, didn't he? Am I about to be fired?

A tightness in her throat, Claudia watched Michael Walsh pause to talk with the two display men still debating about placement of their cut-outs.

But his eyes are on me.

'He's pissed,' Fran warned. 'How did they creep up on us without our hearing them?'

Defiance in her voice now. 'I didn't say anything that wasn't true.' Claudia struggled for calm. Todd's oft-repeated warning darted across her mind:

'Dammit, Claudia! Why must you always say what you think? That's not the way to get ahead in this world.'

'He's coming back.' Alarm in Fran's voice. 'Let's start checking sizes on the Katherine Miller dress rack.'

Michael Walsh strode to where the two women were fabricating work – pretending to be unaware of his presence.

'Your name?' he asked Claudia. Calmly. Politely.

'Claudia Adams.' *He's firing me. What'll I tell the kids?*

'I'm Michael Walsh,' he told her. 'When are you scheduled to go to lunch?'

'At noon.' Her voice was uneven. *He's letting me have half a day of work before he fires me? That's being a 'compassionate' boss?*

'Meet me at the Oasis,' he ordered. His tone brisk. Impersonal. 'Our restaurant on the fifth floor. We need to talk. Oh, if I'm not there just yet, tell the hostess to put you at my table.'

'Right.' Fran was watching them, Claudia thought, as though this was a scene from a suspenseful movie.

Claudia returned to checking sizes on the dress rack, though thus far not one size was out of order.

Fran waited until Walsh had rejoined his entourage, was out of hearing.

'What the hell was that all about?'

'Maybe he takes a soft approach in firing,' Claudia flipped. Refusing to show alarm.

'An expensive approach. Lunch at the Oasis can run to almost thirty bucks.' But Fran appeared intrigued by this unorthodox development. 'And everybody knows he brown-bags it.'

'Firing is a business expense. He signs a tab. It costs him nothing.' Claudia shrugged. One of those girls in the employment office the day she registered had said he 'sticks his nose in everything.'

Eight

A t five minutes before noon Claudia stood at the entrance to the Oasis. It exuded the aura of an expensive restaurant. She glanced inside. No sight of Michael Walsh.

'Yes?' A rather condescending hostess approached her. Claudia's name-tag identified her as a store sales associate. Not the usual Oasis patron.

'Michael Walsh's table, please,' Claudia said, as though about to join a friend at Michael's or the Four Seasons. *He did call down for a table, didn't he?*

'Oh.' The hostess seemed both startled and curious. 'This way, please.'

The Oasis was softly lighted. The booths upholstered in a beige leather that matched the wood paneling. The beige carpeting was plush. Fresh flowers on each table. At the moment two women were the sole occupants.

The hostess presented her with a menu and departed. A waiter appeared with a pair of glasses and a pitcher of water.

'Would you like coffee or tea while you're waiting?' he asked, noting the table was set for two.

'Decaf, please.'

She reached for the menu, began to read. Her eyebrows rose in eloquent response. Hardly the prices a department-store shopper would expect. A carafe of coffee would be billed at a few cents less than three dollars – and to that cost, her budget-minded brain computed, must be added tax and tip. She recalled ten-dollar lunches – fourteen if she chose to indulge in a dessert – in earlier years at Miller's.

Their waiter arrived with her carafe of decaf, poured for her. She sipped with curiosity. Decent coffee – nothing spectacular.

All at once there was a flurry of activity. Three parties of women were being escorted to tables. None carrying parcels? Shoppers from the designer floor – having purchases delivered?

Then Michael Walsh walked into the room. He was being escorted to their table by the hostess.

'I'm sorry to have kept you waiting,' he apologized, sitting across from her.

'It's just a couple of minutes past noon. I have a penchant for being early.' True. Something Todd could never understand.

He gazed at her as though just now seeing her as an individual. 'My obsession, too. I thought I was alone in that these days.' He reached for his menu. 'Let's order, then we'll talk.' But he wasn't reading the menu. He was gazing at her with a quizzical smile. 'How does this place – the Oasis – strike you?'

'Charming,' she conceded.

'And?' he prodded.

'Well, hardly the kind of restaurant that a shopper would expect. It's attractive, pleasant to relax in after heavy shopping. But the prices.' She winced. *Three weeks ago I wouldn't have given it a second thought. So the prices have gone up.* 'It's not as though dining in a department store is a social occasion.' *I'm speaking my mind again – the way Todd used to complain about. Why can't I be diplomatic?*

'What does the typical shopper – and usually it's a woman,' he pointed out, 'expect in a department-store restaurant?'

He's serious – he really wants to know. She thought a moment. 'Women want to rest their feet, assuage their hunger. And most of the time they don't want to linger.' She'd take any bet service here would be painfully slow. Hadn't the menu mentioned that everything was prepared to order?

'You have a marketing background,' he said with an air of discovery.

'My only marketing experience has been shopping for my household. A daughter just out of college, a son in his sophomore year. And occasionally –' irony crept into her voice now – 'shopping for my almost ex-husband.' *I'm talking too much. He's not interested in my family history.* 'Oh, I've set up thrift shops in two cities outside of New York for charitable organizations – and during college years I was a sales clerk –' she paused, chuckled – 'excuse me, sales associate at a small-town boutique.' *He can't expect a marketing degree for the salary Miller pays its sales associates.*

'Let's order lunch,' he said with sudden abruptness.

'Right.' *He isn't comfortable in personal discussions with his employees. But why did he think I had marketing experience?*

A waiter appeared. They focused on ordering. It was clear he lunched here on rare occasions. Still, he appeared interested in every facet of the restaurant's operations. He asked cogent questions of their waiter. The Oasis, she learned, was a franchise.

They both settled on the grilled fillet of salmon and sautéed baby spinach with slivered almonds. The waiter left their table. Michael Walsh gazed at her with questioning eyes.

'Tell me why you disapprove of our – how did you put it?' He squinted in thought. 'Our six foot, anorexic, twenty-year-old models.'

'They put a forty-something or fifty- or sixty- – or even thirty-something,' she added recklessly, 'on the defensive. How many women look like those models? At any age a woman can be attractive, well built – even sexy. Look at the top movie stars – they're not anorexic. I pick up a catalogue – not just Miller's – and I see these young-young faces.' She gestured eloquently.

He pursued questioning her about what he was calling 'the age gap' – and she answered with pithy candor. At last their salmon and spinach arrived. He inspected the picturesque arrangement on the huge plate with a lifted eyebrow.

'Six minutes to grill and twenty to design on the plate.' But he dug into the salmon fillet with the air of a connoisseur. 'It's quite good,' he acknowledged, 'but I like to use a white wine marinade and top the salmon with a walnut crust—'

'Sounds great.' Claudia's face was luminous. This was a subject with which she felt comfortable. 'I usually poach the salmon and serve it with a tarragon sauce and Yukon Gold potatoes. That is, for dinner parties. For family I like something with less fat and fewer calories.'

He gazed at her with an air of amazement.

Isn't a sales associates supposed to know how to cook?

Then all at once he was frowning.

What did I say wrong?

'I need to get back to my office.' He was searching the floor for their waiter. 'I'll ask for a doggie bag and run.' He allowed himself a faint smile. 'But finish your lunch, order dessert. Don't bother with a tip. I'll add it to the tab. And report to my office at nine a.m. tomorrow morning. For the next two weeks you'll be my research assistant. You'll receive a bonus check for those two weeks. Is that all right with you?' At the same time he was summoning their waiter.

'Fine.' She felt lightheaded with relief. *I'm not fired. I'll receive a bonus for the next two weeks.* 'I'll see you at nine a.m. tomorrow.'

But as he strode from the restaurant – doggie bag in hand – she was conscious of a new anxiety. *What kind of research does he mean for me to do? Can I handle it? Did I give him the impression that I was truly business oriented? What is he expecting of me?*

Nine

Churning with impatience Michael waited for an 'up' elevator to arrive. Part of his mind was aware of the impressive cluster of shoppers waiting with him. The discount coupons brought in bargain hunters – but they weren't alone in the discount coupon scene. Lord & Taylor did it regularly. So did Macy's. Not for one instant was he able to forget that Miller's might be on the chopping block if he was unable to bolster the bottom line.

Why the hell did I dash out of the Oasis that way? I could have stayed, relaxed a bit over coffee and dessert. Nothing earth-shattering demanded my presence in my office. Like Dolores is always telling me – I need to learn to unwind.

It was that woman – Claudia Adams. Sitting there with her I could almost believe I could have a real life. She's divorced – I'm divorced. She's lovely, bright – and she's been badly hurt. But what could I give her? I'm under a life sentence – unless I win a huge lottery.

The elevator slid to a stop, disgorged several passengers. He was aware of a pair of furtive glances as he waited for the crowd to pile into the elevator. They probably figured he was a sales associate returning from his lunch hour – or maybe a display person, he thought with a touch of humor. Not for him the two-thousand-dollar suits of a high-ranking company executive.

'You can't sit still through a decent lunch,' Dolores scolded him as he hurried past her desk to his office. 'There's nothing pressing until three o'clock.'

He stared blankly for a moment. 'Damn, those two characters from the main office,' he remembered. 'Bring me last quarter's figures – I'll go over them before they show.'

They were expecting some colossal new campaign – something to resurrect the store to its old status. He felt a tightness between his shoulderblades as he considered this. He'd been here almost four months. He'd made substantial improvements. But they wanted more if the store was to remain open.

His mind began to form the words to sell the Big Boys on a new approach. Serious training of the sales staff had been a big – overdue – step. Just walking through the sales floors he could feel the change in atmosphere. But they weren't alone in this – other stores had done the same. Now he needed more magic.

Was he overestimating what Claudia Adams could add to the mix? Was he allowing his personal feelings – about her as a woman – to color his decision to bring her into the campaign? But he was committed to working with her for only two weeks. He'd know by then what magic she could provide.

This is a business arrangement – nothing more.

Claudia lingered over dessert and coffee – noting that the second cup in the fancy carafe was cold. Almost with an air of defiance she ate slowly, enjoying the time off from the selling floor. Fran had teased her about returning from lunch fifteen or twenty minutes early.

'Claudia, what are you trying to prove? We're entitled to an hour lunch break.'

Still, she was approaching her department ten minutes before she was scheduled to return. At the register, ringing up a sale,

Fran froze for an instant as she approached. Eyebrows lifted in question.

'I've not been fired,' she whispered, sliding her purse in its usual resting place. 'More later.'

From noon to 2 p.m. was the period when those on lunch breaks frequently shopped. Not until well past 2 o'clock was Fran able to pelt Claudia with questions.

'He likes you,' Fran drawled when she'd exhausted her questioning. 'He's single, you know.'

'He's looking for angles to bring to business,' Claudia dismissed. 'Sometimes I talk more than I should – but he liked what he heard. And I was right,' she added defensively. 'I'm realistic. They're not courting the average customer the way they should.'

All he really cares about is proving he's a super-salesman. It's a challenge to him. He's obsessive about the business. But there's another side of him that he keeps under lock and key –

'So you've got this special deal for two weeks—' Fran considered this for a moment. 'For two weeks he'll pick your brains. Then he'll dump you back into the sales-associate pool.'

'Fran, he didn't fire me. And I had a great lunch,' Claudia flipped. 'I'm ahead of the game.'

Claudia heard the phone ringing as she unlocked her apartment door. The two-lock deal endemic in Manhattan. She rushed inside – not bothering to lock, reached for the phone.

'Hello.'

'It's me, Mom.' Jill's voice greeted her. 'I had to go home to change for a business cocktail party and I picked up the mail. There was a letter addressed to you.' She paused. 'From somewhere down in South America. Shall I open it?'

'Of course.' Claudia was conscious of the pounding of her heart. It had to be some word from Todd. But he couldn't be in trouble if he was out of the country. No, it was something about the divorce. *Why is it taking Jill so long to read?*

50

'There's a note—' Hostility in her voice. 'And some papers. The divorce papers,' Jill confirmed.

'What does the note say?' Todd was out of reach of prosecution. And he had some woman caring for his financial needs.

'It just says, "Hi, Claudia. Here are the divorce papers. Sign, have notarized, and return immediately. The divorce will be final ninety days after being filed."'

'I'll sign and have the papers notarized.' No expensive lawyer's fees to encounter here. 'I'll send them right back.' Twenty-two years of their lives written off with a signature.

'Mom, are you okay?'

'I'm fine. When can I pick up the papers? I know your crazy schedule—'

'You'll be working your regular hours tomorrow?' Jill asked.

'Sure.' Later she'd tell Jill about her two-week special assignment.

'I'll drop by the store and give them to you. Some time late in the afternoon,' Jill told her. 'I have to run now. I'm at this cocktail party in a client's townhouse. I took a minute out to call you.' She sounded anxious. 'Mom, you're sure you're all right with this?'

'I'm fine. It's good to have it over.'

Off the phone, Claudia remembered to lock the door. She wasn't fine. Absurdly, she was shaken at the finality of her marriage. Why? she taunted herself. It hadn't been a real marriage for a lot of years.

Delaying dinner preparations, she kicked off her shoes and stretched out on the living room sofa. She'd always been so dubious when other women talked about how husbands could change in the course of a marriage. But Todd had changed. God, had he changed!

Out of college they'd both been so idealistic. They'd yearned to go out and make the world a better place in which to live. They'd talked about joining the Peace Corps. But then she got pregnant, and their whole world changed.

By the time Jill was five, Todd had become a stranger to

her. His whole approach to life had changed. In the back of her mind she'd recognized this, she realized in recall. But she'd blocked it out.

People do change. I lived with a stranger.

With a sudden compulsion for activity she left the sofa and went into the tiny kitchen to prepare a quick dinner. Michael Walsh had talked about grilling salmon and topping it with a walnut crust. Why did he feel uncomfortable talking about cooking? Did he feel it wasn't macho?

No, it doesn't fit his image of the top-level business entrepreneur. He doesn't see me as a woman. I'm somebody who just might have a few ideas to help him rescue Miller's Manhattan from oblivion.

Ten

In her usual compulsive fashion Claudia strode through Miller's Manhattan's personnel premises at 8:40 a.m., though she was scheduled to arrive at 9 a.m. Feeling self-conscious about the day ahead. What kind of research am I scheduled to do? Will I blow it?

The area was deserted except for the woman at a desk just outside Michael Walsh's office. She glanced up from her computer with a smile.

'You must be Claudia. I'm Dolores, Michael's secretary. You're bright and early.'

'Hi, Dolores—' Claudia hesitated, uneasy. 'Am I too early?'

Dolores chortled. 'Nobody's ever too early for Michael. He's here at the crack of dawn. I breeze in about eight or eight fifteen. Go right in – he'll throw work at you before you can sit down.'

Her smile shaky, Claudia approached the door to Michael Walsh's office, knocked lightly.

'Come in.' An absentminded quality in his voice. *Did he forget he told me to come in this morning? Was this just a momentary whim and he's dismissed it already?*

Claudia walked inside with a tentative smile. He glanced up from his cluttered desk.

'You can tell time,' he approved. 'Sit down. Let's go to work.'

'Right.'

In minute detail he went over her remarks about the models used by the store, her pithy diagnosis of the Oasis. *He understood what I was trying to say – and he thinks it's worth following up.*

'I'm talking with the model agency people and the catalogue people. That's in work. I think you hit a nerve there.' He squinted in thought. 'We've focused on one age group – that's a serious mistake. Not every shopper visualizes herself as a twenty-year-old anorexic model. We must diversify. I earlier arranged for music to be piped in on the third floor – I think that's a practical move.'

The third floor catered to the teenagers and early twenty-somethings.

'That's being done in other leading department stores.' She hesitated, fearful of being too aggressive. 'It might be pleasant to have music piped into the fifth-floor ladies' lounge,' she suggested. 'Not rock,' she said with a hint of laughter. 'Maybe Gershwin, Cole Porter—'

'The two greats,' he murmured with infinite respect, then made a swift return to the hardworking entrepreneur image. 'I'll make a note of it.' He scribbled on a note pad, turned to her again. 'In the course of the next two weeks I want you to lunch in every department store restaurant in Manhattan. Then lunch in restaurants close to these stores that might attract shoppers.' He chuckled. 'I don't expect you to eat two or three lunches a day – nibble. You're not anorexic—' His eyes rested on her in approval for an instant, then he thrust himself back into business. 'But see what they're serving. Make notes of the prices – how fast is the service. The reactions of the women. I know – we have a men's department,' he conceded, 'but it's the women shoppers who keep us afloat.' He paused in thought for a moment. 'Check on restaurants and snack bars in the major discount stores, also. Let's get the whole picture.'

She listened in rapt attention while he explained how she was to handle her expense account. All the while her mind outlined the department stores where she was to dine. Start with the better ones, she exhorted herself. The competition for Miller's Manhattan.

'You're computer literate?' he asked in sudden doubt.

'Yes,' she told him.

'All right, I'll have Dolores assign you a cubicle with a computer.' He reached for a buzzer on his desk. 'I'll expect a written nightly report.'

'Right.'

'Work up the list of department stores to tackle, get on it. I think this can be covered in two weeks.'

'Yes.' The number of department stores in Manhattan had dropped shockingly in the past few years.

'Start with the Oasis,' he continued. 'We just talked there. You didn't have a chance to focus on its operation.'

'Sure.' *He's dismissing me. I'm one tiny cog in his campaign to bring Miller's Manhattan out of the red.*

Claudia sat at a table in the Oasis and lingered over coffee – allowing herself to tune in to the conversations at surrounding tables. Searching for reactions to the restaurant. Noting the many empty tables.

She'd be eating well these two weeks, she thought with a flicker of humor. Dinner would be cereal, a piece of fruit, and herb tea. Little clean-up afterwards.

Now she reached into her purse for a notebook and pen. A month ago the pricey menu here would not have disturbed her. She winced as she tabulated the cost of her luncheon. The carafe of coffee was $2.95 – add sales tax and a 20% tip, and that would be pushing $4.00 for coffee alone. Her lunch altogether – with tip – approached $30.00. Not exactly a shopper's lunch.

Now she tuned in to the conversation between a waiter and a new arrival.

'You don't just have sandwiches?' A new arrival asked. Shocked at the prices, Claudia interpreted compassionately.

'We have the free-range chicken sandwich.' The waiter pointed to a line on the menu. 'Perhaps you'd like to bypass the coffee?'

'Yes,' the young woman said with an air of relief. 'The turkey sandwich on rye toast, please – and a glass of water.'

So there was resistance to the prices. The wait staff was conscious of this – and disturbed by it. Miller's – like most department stores – was fighting for customer dollars. But many customers coming in to shop with their 15% or 20% discount coupons weren't likely to be pleased with the tab in either of the store's restaurants. The sandwich and coffee she'd had earlier at the store's Light Lunch Corner had cost roughly $14.00. A dessert would have added $6.00. Not exactly customer-friendly.

Belatedly she remembered that Jill had said she'd be dropping by the store with the divorce papers this afternoon. She was conscious of a sudden chill. How easily Todd had tossed twenty-two years of marriage out the window.

But she had the kids – Jill and Larry made those years important. They were so sweet, so loving. They were furious with Todd, wanted no part of him. She was startled at intervals to realize how little she missed Todd in her life. For the past fifteen years she'd been playing a role dictated by him. No, she thought defiantly, there was no moaning at the bar for the end of this marriage.

She forced her mind back into the present. Call Jill, tell her to leave the papers with Fran. Give her instructions. Later she'd explain about this two-week assignment.

What kind of bonus was Michael Walsh talking about?

Anything additional to her paycheck would be welcome. She wasn't to touch Larry's college money – no matter how tight the situation.

All right, go back to the office. Type up the first two restaurant reports, hand them in. Then head for the Mid-Manhattan Library to research the books catalogue and the microfilm for the inner workings of a nursery school – with the thought that a nursery project for shoppers might be a good addition. A lot to accomplish, she warned herself in sudden realization of what lay ahead.

In two weeks she'd be shifted back to the selling floor. Michael Walsh was adept at picking brains, she warned herself. And just as adept at tossing the current brain back into the heap.

Is there some way I can work up from a holiday selling job to something more substantial? Can I promote this two-week campaign into a full-time job? It could be exciting to work with Michael Walsh on a regular basis.

But all at once she was unnerved. It wasn't the prospect of working in this new field that she found exciting. It was Michael Walsh.

There's no room in my life for a man. Twenty-two years of marriage is enough for a lifetime.

Claudia was startled to realize it was almost 6 p.m. when she emerged from the Mid-Manhattan Library with an armful of books and a batch of copies from the microfilm files. So much for the 9 a.m. to 5 p.m. working hours on this assignment, she derided wryly.

Had Fran left the store yet? she asked herself in sudden concern. Jill must have given her the divorce papers. She felt a compulsive need to have them on their way back to Todd.

She hurried the few blocks to the store, rushed up to their floor. Fran was still there, she noted with relief.

'Your daughter looks just like you,' Fran greeted her. 'And she wears gorgeous clothes.'

56

'She gave you the papers?' Claudia's throat felt tight. *So the divorce is in work. Let it be over, this phoney marriage.*

'They're in my purse. Have dinner with me,' Fran invited. 'My treat. I got a huge tip from this UN guy who bought my oversized cheesecake yesterday. We'll eat Chinese,' she added. 'That's within my budget.'

'I'd like that—' Tonight – with the divorce papers to sign – it would be good not to eat alone. 'But I have to run to Michael's office and type up my report—' She was ambivalent now.

'So it's Michael now,' Fran drawled.

'Everybody calls him Michael.' All at once Claudia was self-conscious. *Why is Fran making it sound like something it isn't?* 'It'll take me about ten minutes—'

'I won't be out of here for another thirty minutes. Go. We'll eat Chinese.'

Claudia walked through the deserted personnel office to the rear suite. Dolores sat before her computer with an air of tension.

'Michael's been in conference for two hours with the Big Boys,' she reported.

She's worried about what's happening. They won't fire Michael? But I'd still go back to the sales floor – until after Christmas. Is Dolores worried about her own job? This is a rotten time to go job-hunting.

'Type up your report in the morning,' Dolores told her. 'You've put in enough hours for today.'

It was awful the way people feared losing their jobs, Claudia thought – heading for the 'down' escalator. Dolores was scared Michael would be fired – and she'd go with him. Fran was terrified – though she made a strong effort to conceal it – that Miller's Manhattan might be closed. *I might be transferred to the White Plains store – but I might not.*

Was it Thoreau who said, 'Most people live lives of quiet desperation.'

Eleven

Claudia and Fran sat at a rear table in the tiny Chinese restaurant close to Fran's East 50s studio apartment.

'This is my favorite "dinner out" place,' Fran said. 'I figured you'd like it. My "health-food nut" friend,' she joshed. The restaurant boasted that all vegetables were steamed without oil, corn starch, or msg. Brown rice was served.

'Everything's great.' Claudia dug into her vegetables – topped with scallops – with gusto. She glanced about the room. ' The place is filling up.' Not surprising, considering the prices. And the staff was warm and ingratiating, the service fast.

'The family that owns it lives in terror of the day their lease runs out.' Fran sighed. 'So many small businesses can't deal with the escalating rents. Oh, it's not just in housing – businesses are being beat up, too.'

Claudia winced. 'In three and a half months I'll be looking for an apartment. My sublet runs out then,' she explained.

'My older niece – she's twenty-two and fresh out of college – flew the coop. She was frank. She said how could she live at home and have a relationship? So she found herself this tiny studio in Brooklyn Heights – and sweats to pay the rent.'

'With Jill's insane hours she has no time for a relationship. She's on a fast track as a systems analyst. The company takes on a batch of young people fresh out of college, works them seventy hours a week, chooses a handful at the end of two years and chucks the others out. When – in that kind of schedule – would Jill have time for a relationship?'

'She'll get over that.' Fran dismissed this. 'Women always find time for a relationship. If they want it.' She shrugged. 'I played for a while – when I was younger. Nobody showed that I wanted to spend the rest of my life with. I don't mind living alone,' she added with candor. 'I have to cater to nobody but myself. I read a lot – courtesy of the public library system.' She shuddered. 'My budget doesn't allow for the price of books – not in the quantity I read.'

'I worry about making it from check to check,' Claudia admitted. 'I go into the supermarket and face shock at the checkout counter. How do single mothers with a couple of kids manage on the salaries we're seeing?'

'They eat a lot of pasta, ration fruit, buy chicken when it's on sale. And try for second jobs.' Fran inspected her with friendly curiosity. 'You never went through that routine?'

'No.' She forced a smile. 'But I'm there now. Why is it always the woman whose living standard goes down with divorce?'

'Everybody on our sales floor is fascinated by the way you and Michael Walsh clicked.' A glint in Fran's eyes.

'Fran, you've been reading romance novels,' Claudia accused. 'I made a statement that sent signals popping up in his brain. Business signals,' she added because of Fran's chuckle. 'All that man cares about is showing how great he is at saving failing stores. I hit a nerve with him.' She shrugged. 'So for two weeks I'm eating like a high roller in Vegas – and I'll get a special bonus. And at the end of two weeks Cinderella will be back on the selling floor.'

Why do I feel attracted to him? The old rebound deal? There's no room in my life for a man. Besides, history proves – my choices are rotten.

Claudia was preparing for bed when Larry called.

'Just checking up on you,' he drawled. 'You okay, Mom?'

'I'm fine. You sound as though you have a cold—' *But he can go to the school infirmary, can't he?*

'Half the school has colds.' Larry shrugged this off. 'It's

that time of year.' Now he cleared his throat in the familiar way that said he was about to broach a delicate subject. 'Mom, are you sure you can handle the next semester here?'

'The money is in a special account. You'll finish your sophomore year there. In the spring we'll worry about next year.' *Poor baby, it was a shock to him to realize he had to switch schools midstream. But Todd went to a state college. So did I. How many families can afford Ivy League and Seven Sisters fees?* She shuddered, recalling how fees kept escalating year after year.

'How's the job?' Larry asked.

He feels uncomfortable about my working. 'I'm on a special assignment for two weeks,' she said lightly and filled him in.

'My mother the marketing executive.' He chortled. 'Maybe you ought to go back to school for an MBA—' He broke off, as though in sudden recognition of their financial state.

'It's only for two weeks. This high-powered entrepreneur will pick my brains for two weeks, then dump me for somebody else. But for two weeks it's fun.' *Play it light – I don't want Larry worrying about me.* 'But let's not run up a big phone bill for you, darling. And take care of that cold.'

Claudia arrived at the store at minutes past 8 a.m. She hurried to the personnel floor, through the avenue of empty desks to where Dolores sat frowning at her computer monitor.

'Good morning, Dolores.'

'I have a love-hate relationship with my computer,' Dolores greeted Claudia. 'When it works, I love it. When there's trouble, I hate it. Go on in,' she said without a break. 'He's waiting to talk with you.'

'Sure.' *Did I do something wrong?*

She rushed to hang away her coat, to thrust her purse into her desk drawer, and reached for the report she'd written yesterday.

The door to Michael's office was open. She hesitated at the entrance.

'Good morning—'

'Good morning.' He frowned, as though greetings were a waste of time. 'Sit down and let's go over what you've dug up on a proposed day-nursery situation.'

'I've just come up with the basics so far—' A note of apology in her voice. 'The ratio of teachers to children, the insurance that would be required. The necessary space – I believe it's controlled by a city agency.' *Is he sorry he gave me the go-ahead to spend time on this?*

'Tell me why you believe it'll increase our traffic,' he ordered. 'Who will it bring into the store?' He leaned forward – almost accusingly, she thought. Or was it just that he was so intense about whatever he approached?

'Women with young children. Women with comfortable incomes but not to the point where they hire nannies. Stay-at-home moms. Anywhere from mid-twenties to mid-forties. Women are having children in their later years these days.' *Does he have children? Does his ex-wife have custody? He's warm and charismatic – he'd be a good father.*

'I don't have any kids,' he said as though reading her mind. 'Except a daughter for about five minutes. She died at birth.' *Even now he grieves for her. How sad.*

'I'm sorry—'

'All right.' He was back in the familiar mode. 'Why will the nursery help us?'

'Give the prospective shoppers an hour – possibly two – to make their selections without their attention being diverted to kids. They'll feel free to focus on making selections. With a child or two in tow they can become impatient, dismiss something they might otherwise buy.'

'It could be an expensive experiment,' he said after a moment. 'But it has possibilities.' He leaned back in his chair, closed his eyes, swore under his breath when his phone rang.

Off the phone, he turned back to Claudia. 'Are you clear to work this evening?' he asked briskly. 'It'll be considered overtime,' he added with a faint smile.

'Yes—'

'I'd like to work away from any possible interruptions. That can happen here.' His voice was dry. 'Let's have dinner together at my place. I'll put the phone off the hook, and we can dig seriously into this project.' Unexpectedly he chuckled. 'If you can put up with my cooking—'

'No problem,' she shrugged. *Fran would say, "He's getting ideas!" No way – he's all business.*

Twelve

Claudia spent two hours at the Mid-Manhattan Library, broke for her lunch research, then returned to the library. At the store again, she stopped by the sales floor to talk for a few moments with Fran. Self-conscious about the evening's work session, she avoided mentioning this. So Michael Walsh was an unconventional boss. There would be nothing personal about their working at his apartment.

Still, she felt an odd excitement as she walked to the door of his office at a few moments before 6 p.m. He said they'd be leaving around then. Was it her imagination or was there a speculative gleam in Dolores' eyes when he emerged from his office and indicated they were to leave?

'Call it a day, Dolores,' he joshed. 'You're always yelling at me for being a workhorse.'

The rest of the office floor had already signed out. They walked to the bank of elevators, waited for a 'down' car. The store would be open for another hour. Claudia was conscious of furtive stares as they walked through the street-level floor to the revolving doors that led to the chilly night. All the while Michael was shooting questions at her about her day's restaurant experience.

'We'll cab up to my place,' Michael said, an arm already raised to signal an available cab. 'I'm in the West 70s,' he told her. 'It's a quick subway ride. But it'll be faster by cab.' And to Michael, she interpreted, time was valuable.

While they drove up to his building, he talked almost obsessively about the need to rescue Miller's Manhattan.

'There're a lot of jobs at stake.' He was somber. *He's truly concerned about people.* 'It's shocking to consider how many stores have given up the fight. If the bottom line isn't healthy, it's the end of the line.'

'Even after all these years I hear women talk wistfully about Altman's having closed,' Claudia recalled. 'Tourists coming into the city miss it.'

'The concept of vertical shops – which is basically what a department store is – will come around again,' he mused. 'But meanwhile I worry about all the jobs being lost. And that's in addition to all the jobs being exported.'

'I can't understand how anyone can say our economy is good when so many are unemployed.' A rebellious glint in Claudia's eyes now. 'So many being forced to take jobs at half their previous salaries. The economy is good for big business,' she summed up. 'Not for working families.'

'We're moving into a two-class society.' His face was taut with rejection. 'Those who have, and those who have not.'

He lived in a tall, pre-war building. Once, she surmised, it would have been considered a luxury building. The doorman greeted him with a warm smile. He was probably a good tipper.

'This is a rent-stabilized building,' he told her while they rode up to his 6th-floor apartment. 'I've been here almost nine years – since before Manhattan rents went totally insane. And the building never went co-op.'

'I'm in a short-term sublet – also stabilized. My daughter lives in a new building with an insane rent.' Claudia sighed. 'And has what I consider an insane job. She works about seventy hours a week.' *I shouldn't have said that. Michael works 70-hour weeks.*

'The paycheck can be a mighty incentive.' A touch of cynicism in his smile.

She waited with a tense smile while Michael unlocked the routine two locks, pushed the door wide. Her first glance about the apartment noted the spartan furnishing. For Michael this was just a place to sleep. She doubted he'd lived here with his wife.

But savory aromas were emerging from the galley kitchen similar to her own. This was another world from the rest of the apartment, she surmised. An impressive crockpot sat on the counter. An attractive array of flame Le Creuset sat on a decorative wrought-iron rack. An impressive collection of copper pots and pans hung from the ceiling.

'Whatever's cooking has to be great.' She sniffed in approval while Michael inspected the contents of the crockpot.

'It's been cooking – very low – for eleven hours.'

He seems another person here in the kitchen. Here his tension disappears. He radiates a sense of peace.

'My variation on Chicken Casablanca. It's all in the choice of spices.'

'It sounds great.' Michael could concoct gourmet food in this tiny kitchen, she thought with admiration – remembering her elaborate oversized kitchen in the townhouse.

'Bring down plates while I steam the rice,' he ordered, pointing to a cabinet. 'The silver is in the drawer there—'

'Right.' The dishes were limited in number, she noted, but of fine, delicate china. *He shopped at Tiffany's for two place settings – expensive but beautiful.* The silver, too, was lovely. She was conscious of an unexpected serenity as she set the small table in the dining area.

'Regular coffee or decaf?' he asked while he transferred chicken from crockpot to serving plate.

'Decaf.'

'The beans – decaf – are in the fridge.' He nodded towards the grinder. 'Grind them and start the coffee maker while I bring out the salad.'

'Sure.' *Most men – living alone – would settle for instant.*

They moved about the tiny kitchen as a team. Without prodding Claudia checked the rice. It was hot enough to serve. In minutes they were at the small dining table and digging into the savory crockpot chicken.

'What did you add to the chicken before you brought it to the table?' Claudia was curious but approving.

'Parsley and cilantro,' he told her while she ate with gusto.

'You'll be eating this for the next three nights,' she surmised. 'Or you'll freeze for other nights.'

'I'll have it tomorrow night, freeze what's left for next week.' His eyes grew reminiscent. 'When I remember some of the meals I've eaten in the past.' He chuckled in recall. 'I spent twenty-seven months with the Peace Corps in Africa – when I was fresh out of college.'

Claudia stared at him in disbelief. 'My ex-husband and I talked about joining the Peace Corps right out of college.' *We could have been there at the same time.* 'Our parents were alarmed, persuaded us to wait. Then I got pregnant – and it was too late.' Her mind darted back through the years. 'It's amazing how people change. Five years later Todd wouldn't believe we'd talked about joining the Peace Corps. The last half of my marriage I felt as though I was living with a stranger.'

'I haven't seen my ex-wife in almost eleven years,' Michael said slowly. 'I've spoken to her three times in that period. Twice when I mailed her alimony check three days late, and once when her check was lost in the mail. Living alone has its advantages.' A defiant tone in his voice.

He sounds as though he's trying to convince himself.

'We cater only to ourselves.'

But he's lonely – he feels something's lacking in his life.

All at once Claudia felt an overwhelming need to re-channel their conversation. 'If I tried to get involved with the Peace Corps now, my kids would have heart attacks. They'd be terrified for me. They're good kids,' she said with a blend of love and pride.

'I never had a chance to know my daughter,' he said after a moment. 'She died a few minutes after birth. But then I tell myself, "Everything in life comes with a price-tag. I've missed the joy of having kids – but I've missed the tough times, too."' All at once he seemed self-conscious.

'All right, tell me about the nursery deal,' he prodded. 'I may run into opposition at the main office. It'll be expensive.'

'But consider the masses of publicity it could bring – with the right push,' she pursued.

Now they focused on dissecting in minute detail the data Claudia had accumulated in her research. *I'm not here just to enjoy this terrific dinner – this is a working session.* Yet at errant moments she was conscious of unnerving undercurrents. He was seeing her as something more than an employee on the job.

With chicken and salad eaten, Michael leaned back in thought. 'The best approach would be to use the nursery situation at specific, heavy sales periods. Such as between Thanksgiving and New Year's,' he finally concluded. 'Too late for this year – but something to consider for the future.'

'That sounds realistic,' she agreed. *But I won't be around to see it.*

Michael seemed in some inner debate. Claudia rose from the table, went into the kitchen to pour coffee for them. She hesitated about bringing out milk, remembered he'd had his coffee black when they'd lunched together at the store.

'Work up a presentation on the nursery project that I can present to the main office,' he told her as he reached for his coffee.

Can I do that? He trusts me do it?

'Stress that this is not just a proposal for Miller's Manhattan but for the entire chain.'

He'll be stepping on toes. It'll sound as though he's trying to move up into more rarified territory.

'I'll mention your involvement in the campaign.' His eyes searched hers now. Disconcerting in their intensity.

'Thank you.' She managed a faint smile.

Why am I feeling this way about a man I met a little over two weeks ago? As though my life is about to take a new and exciting path. Oh, this is insane! Get a grip, Claudia. Keep your feet on the ground!

Thirteen

Claudia was conscious of a reluctance in Michael to end their 'working session.' They had consumed an astonishing amount of decaf as they explored the day-nursery project. Then he'd apologized for not having served a dessert.

'I lead a spartan life,' he apologized with a wry smile – echoing her impression of his apartment. 'Would you settle now for what I call my semi-guilt-free dessert? Low-fat coffee yogurt splashed with Kahlua liqueur?'

'It sounds great.' Emotions unfelt in years welled in her. *Our mouths say one thing and our eyes say something else.*

Returning from the kitchen with their belated dessert – seeming slightly unnerved - Michael switched to the subject of the store restaurants, what changes would be effective.

'What about a cafeteria?' he asked. 'Quick service, inexpensive. Not the cold, antiseptic types of years ago. An attractive room, soft music—'

'No,' she rejected. 'Women who've shopped are tired. They want to sit down – maybe kick off their shoes under the table. They need space for their parcels. They don't want to try to juggle shopping bags and trays.'

'You're right, of course.'

I don't want to end this evening, either. This is what experts warn divorced women against – a deadly rebound.

All at once she was conscious of an abrupt withdrawal in him. 'It's late. I'll put you in a cab. Get a receipt from the driver – it goes on your expense account.'

Michael flipped on the radio. A program of classical music filtered into the air. Now he went into the kitchen to stack the dishwasher. For the first time since he'd moved into this apartment, he'd entertained a guest. All right, it was a business session. Technically it was business session.

How empty the apartment seemed, now that Claudia was gone. From what little she'd said, he gathered she was going through an ugly divorce. She'd intimated as much. But there was a chemistry between them – something he'd never experienced before.

Was I wrong in sensing she feels something for me? Can that happen in such a short time? But what can there ever be for us? I've said it ever since the divorce – I'm in thrall to Lisa. I'm married to my job.

Returning the kitchen to its normal neatness, he allowed his mind to roam into areas normally avoided. All he'd ever wanted was to open a small restaurant. One that catered to people who recognized fine dining, yet sought a healthful approach. Not to cook himself but to organize the perfect staff. Hell, Dad had been right, of course. Running a restaurant was a huge gamble – and where would he ever find the financial backing? Put the dream back to bed.

Leaving the kitchen he knew this would be another night when sleep would be elusive. He went through the usual nightly routine, lay back against the pillows – conscious of every city sound. The raucous garbage truck just below, the boom box in a passing car, an ambulance shrieking through the night street. His body a tyrant.

Tonight – sitting at the table across from Claudia – he'd envisioned a life that might have been for them.

I'm so damned tired of playing games with myself!

Pretending I love the challenge of moving ahead in the field, fighting to rise into the top echelon – with huge bucks. So it happens it won't be the life I envisioned for myself.

Unlocking her apartment door, Claudia heard her answering machine repeating its recorded message. She rushed to pick up.

'Hello—' Breathless from haste.

'Hi, Mom,' Jill greeted her. 'I know it's late but—'

'Darling, for you it's midday,' Claudia joshed. 'How are you?'

'I thought you'd be pleased – I'm getting an apartment-sharer—'

But Claudia was conscious of a guarded quality in her voice. 'Fine. But you don't sound enthusiastic—'

'It's kind of unconventional. At least, it may seem that way to you—'

'She's a stripper?' *Why do kids always think their mothers are a generation behind them in their thinking?*

'She's a "he".' Jill was blunt. 'But Chris is gay,' she rushed to explain. 'So there's no problem.'

'How did you find him?' Truantly her mind dashed back to the John Ritter TV series of earlier years. The Ritter character had pretended to be gay.

'Sandy is back home in Boston now – and she was talking with Teresa Taylor, who was at school with us. Terry's brother Chris was just excessed from his Internet job. He hated it, but it had sounded promising. But once he was unemployed he decided to move to New York and look for a low-level publishing job because that's a field that excites him.'

'If he's unemployed, what'll he use for rent money?' Claudia forced herself to be practical. 'Or is his family willing to support him?'

'A friend wangled this job for him. Teresa said he's been fascinated by books since he was twelve. It's a low-level job, but he wants to learn the business from the bottom up. He has

69

to report for work next Monday – he was desperate for a place to live. And Sandy's leaving the furniture behind. Most of it was from IKEA – it wasn't a major investment. She knows Chris – he's bright and sweet and—'

'Hold it,' Claudia interrupted. 'In a low-level job he'll be able to pay your kind of rent?' She was skeptical.

'Sandy had a long talk with him. He'll have to draw on his savings until he gets a raise – but he won't have to buy furniture so he can handle it—'

'And he's sure he'll get a raise fast,' Claudia picked up. *The young are optimistic. Remember us at college graduation?* 'What if he doesn't get a raise – and his savings are gone?'

'So he'll be able to hang on for six months.' Jill shrugged this off. 'For the next six months I won't have to worry.'

I'll worry. But the crazy rental market creates weird sharing arrangements. These are difficult times. Jill is being practical. She's working insanely hard – but she's receiving a substantial paycheck on a regular basis.

'It's not an ideal situation,' Claudia hedged. *Where will I be living when Laura returns from Iraq? It's scary. Will I find a job after Christmas?*

'Mom, you know the crazy rental in the city these days—'

Off the phone with Jill, Claudia hesitated a moment. It was late to be calling Shirley – but not too late. Once the kids were in bed she and Bill settled down to watch a little TV. Shirley wouldn't mind being pulled away from the TV set.

She punched in Shirley's number, waited.

'Hello.' Shirley's cheery voice greeted her. This must have been a good day – she didn't sound dragged out.

'I know it's late,' Claudia began.

'Honey, not for you,' Shirley scolded.

'I just talked with Jill. You know the craziness with her apartment—'

'Sure—'

'Well, she's found a roommate. I gather he'll be moving in over the weekend.'

70

'He?' An electric quality in Shirley's voice. 'Jill's going into a relationship?'

'No. He's gay – Theresa Taylor's brother—'

'Oh, I remember Theresa – but she never mentioned a gay brother. But why should she?'

'I feel strange about it,' Claudia admitted. 'And not just because I adored *Three's Company* all those years ago. Jill said Chris Taylor is gay – and I believe it.'

'Claudia, look back at our college years. All those co-ed dorm rooms. We didn't think anything about that.'

'That was different.' Claudia was defensive. 'It was a phase in our culture.'

'A permanent phase.' Shirley dismissed this. 'And hey, it's good to have a man about the house. To change light bulbs, take out the garbage, fix the computer when it goes down—'

'Jill can do that. I can do that. Well, not fix the computer,' Claudia conceded.

'Relax, honey. She won't have to pay that ghastly rent – she'll share it. It's happening all over these days.'

'Todd never changed a light bulb, put out the garbage, did anything about the house,' Claudia recalled, then her face softened. 'Larry did that.'

And now Larry would spend Thanksgiving weekend and the Christmas holidays sleeping on a convertible in her sublet apartment. And worrying about the next two years of college . . .

Fourteen

Despite a near-sleepless night, Claudia arrived at the store minutes past 8 a.m. She found an odd pleasure in walking through the empty store – as though she belonged here. Not just for the brief holiday period.

Was there any chance she'd be kept on after the Christmas madness? No, that was wishful thinking. And in another nine days she'd finish this stint with Michael. How had she come to feel so close to him in such a short while?

Dolores had not yet arrived, she noted. The door to Michael's office was closed. In her cubicle Claudia settled herself at her computer to write up her two reports on yesterday's lunches. In the afternoon, she plotted – after her restaurant research – she'd start work on the day-nursery proposal.

Today she was starkly conscious of the two-week schedule for her role as Michael's assistant. After that she'd be back on the selling floor. Would there be a repetition of last evening's working session at his apartment?

She tried to focus on the work at hand, but at intervals her mind traveled back to last evening's conversation with Jill. She'd tried to be casual about the situation – but she was upset. Hadn't Jill said she'd loathe sharing with a stranger? Jill knew his sister – she'd never met him.

If this craziness with Todd hadn't happened, they'd have the condo. Jill could have arranged for a sublet and returned home. Now she had nowhere to go. Weren't magazine articles constantly talking about young people coming back to the family nest at these times? *But Jill has no family nest.*

Dolores hovered in the doorway. 'You trying to make me look like a slacker?' she teased. 'Only Michael ever beats me in.' A glint of friendly curiosity in her eyes.

She knows we left together last evening. Does she know about the working session at Michael's apartment? 'I wanted to catch up on my restaurant reports,' Claudia told her. 'I left without doing them yesterday.'

'Michael said to ask you to be available for a meeting at three o'clock today,' Dolores reported.

'No problem.' Claudia smiled – hiding a touch of panic that

was closing in on her. *What kind of a meeting? What am I supposed to do?*

'He'll be sitting down with a big wheel from the main office who's flown in for twenty-four hours.' Dolores seemed to be reading her mind. 'He'll be visiting the White Plains store in the morning, then coming here in the afternoon.'

'Should I know what it's about?' Claudia asked. *Michael's got this conviction that I'm a marketing expert. What will he expect me to say?*

'From what Michael said, I gather the guy wants to know what Michael's working on to improve the store's image. He figures as a woman you can be their sounding board.'

'Wow!' Claudia was unnerved.

'You'll do fine,' Dolores soothed. 'You're sharp – Michael sensed that right away. Just say what you think.'

Claudia laughed wryly 'I have a reputation for doing that.' She remembered Larry witnessing her encounter with a wily electrician. *'Mom, you're tough.'*

Michael still hadn't emerged from his office when she left for her first lunch of the day. Between 11:30 a.m. and 2:30 p.m. she'd nibble at three lunches. She'd have ample time to be back at the store by 3 p.m. for Michael's meeting.

Debating about it for a moment, she decided to stop off on their floor to see Fran for a few minutes – if she wasn't busy. She mustn't say anything about last evening, she warned herself. Fran would see it in the wrong light. Still, in a corner of her mind she remembered the unspoken emotions that had engulfed both Michael and herself.

'Hi, you're off to another toney luncheon,' Fran jibed, idle behind the sales desk.

'Two lowdown lunches, then the fancy one,' Claudia told her. 'How're you doing?'

All at once Fran was serious. 'I'm getting strange vibes about my side-business people. I know – people are watching their money these days. But two customers who always come to me for big birthday cakes are cutting this year.'

'It'll change,' Claudia comforted. 'They'll be back.'

'The cake money provides my comfort zone.' Fran shrugged. 'So who am I to be exempt from the drop in lifestyles?'

'Oh, Jill called last night. She's found a roommate.'

'So why do you look disturbed?'

'It's a guy –'

'Ah-hah. A relationship in work?'

'She's never met him – he's a brother of a college friend. And he's gay.'

'So, if he pays the rent what's wrong with it?' Fran demanded. 'You said the apartment has two bedrooms and two baths. I don't see either of them doing much cooking – nor sitting around in the living room.'

'Those rents are scary.' Claudia shuddered. *But the maintenance – including the mortgage - on the condo had been formidable. Only it hadn't seemed like that then.* 'I'd better run – I have work to do.'

'Oh, such labor,' Fran drawled, but the glint in her eyes was sympathetic. 'Enjoy your lunches.'

Claudia had heard Michael greet his three o'clock appointment almost ten minutes ago. Now she could hear the faint hum of voices in Michael's office. He hadn't summoned her as yet. Was she off the hook?

Why do I feel so insecure about meeting these people? I've entertained Todd's top-level business associates with no qualms, though I knew what happened at the dinner table could mean big bucks for Todd. A corporate wife had obligations – and I fulfilled them. Why do I feel so insecure now?

Was it the knowledge that she'd been discarded as a wife? Rejected? What had happened to her ego? Michael had faith in her contribution to the company. In a corner of her mind she kept hoping this would turn into a permanent job. She didn't want to think about after Christmas – when she'd be job hunting again

She paused at the computer – alert to sounds beyond her

74

cubicle. Dolores had left her desk, was going into Michael's office. Michael must have asked for some reports. Now – perversely – she was anxious to be called into that meeting. To prove her worth as an employee.

The phone rang. She waited for an instant. Dolores wasn't picking up. Dolores expected her to do that.

She picked up on the third ring. 'Michael Walsh's office, good afternoon.' Dolores' stock refrain.

'Mom, it's me.' Larry's voice – strained but determined – came to her. 'I've thought about it a lot, and I want to quit school, be practical. I'll be coming in late tonight so—'

'Larry, no!' Claudia was unnerved. 'Under no circumstances are you to drop out of school. I—'

'Mom, it'll be too rough on you,' he protested. 'I can—'

'I would be miserable if you dropped out. You'll get your degree – maybe at a state school – but you'll finish college. I won't hear of anything else. You'll need to get a summer job,' she conceded. 'But you stay in school.'

'Claudia,' Dolores called. 'Michael would like you to join him in his office.'

'Larry, I have to go to a meeting,' she said hastily. 'Call me tonight. But forget this craziness!'

Fifteen

Fighting for poise – contriving the required smile - Claudia walked into Michael's office. Michael sat on the black leather sofa – that on occasional overnighters, Dolores confided, served as his bed – beside a man in his early fifties wearing an expensive Italian suit.

Michael rushed to introduce them. 'Don, this my new assistant, Claudia Adams.' A wary glint in his eyes. She suspected he was anticipating a rough time with the visitor from the main office. *He called me his new assistant.* 'Claudia, this is Don Logan. I'd like you to explain to Don your reaction to our regular catalogue layouts.'

Claudia sat in the matching leather club chair at right angles to the two men and launched into a report. She was conscious of Logan's covert inspection of her designer pantsuit, her Ferragamo pumps. He would recognize the exquisite tailoring of her suit, the fine workmanship of her shoes. In his mind that would catagorize her as a successful business woman.

'It's a rather elementary outlook.' Logan was slightly condescending in tone, but his eyes said he was impressed.

'It's the way women feel. If you've talked with as many women as I have in my research assignments,' she fabricated, 'you'd understand this is a neglected field of thought.'

Logan began to shoot questions at her. She refused to be rattled, replied with answers she'd given Michael. Acting on impulse, she reached for the current Miller's Manhattan catalogue that lay at a corner of the coffee table before the sofa.

'Take this catalogue,' she said with a blend of indulgence and dissatisfaction. 'I'm a typical Miller's Manhattan customer. I'm a forty-three-year-old woman staring at this technicolor, glossy display piece – and what do I see? These young-young models – probably younger than my daughter – in these young-young outfits. Oh, here and there,' she conceded, flipping through the pages, 'is an outfit I might be able to wear. But there's nothing smart – elegant – for the over-forty woman.'

'Young women spend a lot of money,' Logan reminded.

'I'm not saying eliminate these young-young models,' Claudia told him. 'But let's not make them the focal point of every catalogue.'

Michael joined in dissecting this approach. Logan hedged, but Claudia suspected they'd sold this point.

'We'll take it up at a meeting when I return to the main office,' he promised. 'You may have some merit there.' An approach for the entire chain, she guessed – recognizing the glint of satisfaction in Michael's eyes.

Now Michael brought up the subject of seasonal day-nursery care.

'We're speaking of two-hour sessions per patron,' Michael explained. 'To allow her to shop without distractions. It'll be expensive but worth it. Not for this year,' he acknowledged, 'but perhaps for two weeks just before Easter.'

For almost an hour Logan shot questions at both Claudia and Michael. Then he announced he had to head for the White Plains store.

'I'm running behind schedule. This is such a whirlwind trip,' he explained. 'I have to fly home early tomorrow morning. But you two appear to be on to something,' he conceded. 'Wrap it all up in a report and send it out to me.'

Michael waited until the door of his office closed behind their visiting big wheel. They heard him talk for a moment with Dolores, then leave their suite.

'We did it!' he chortled. 'They'll buy the whole package before we're done. Let's try to ship out the reports by first thing next week.'

'No problem.'

'Knock off early today. You've had a rough week,' he said gently. 'But we'll probably be here Saturday,' he warned. 'I expect the catalogue crew to sit down with us then.'

'I'll remind Dolores to check with the modeling agency – to make sure the photos are here by tomorrow afternoon—' She stopped short. *Am I taking on too much? Stepping in Dolores's territory?*

'Yeah, do that.' Michael was behind his desk already, searching through papers.

Claudia stopped for a few moments of chatter with Dolores – slipping in a remark about their needing the photos by tomorrow afternoon, without making it appear an order. Now she settled herself in her cubicle again. Michael's words echoing in her mind: *'Don, this is my new assistant, Claudia Adams.' Am I reading too much into that?*

She waited until close to 6 p.m., when she knew Fran would be leaving for the day. She found Fran in the ladies' lounge.

'It's been a wild day,' she confided with a wry smile.

'I know you're on the very light dinner kick,' Fran said indulgently. 'Why don't we stop in for coffee and a muffin and yak a bit before heading home?'

'Sounds great.' Larry was to call later – but instinct told her it would be well into the evening before he called.

They left the store – noting the influx of early evening customers. Women – mostly women – shopping after a day's work.

'It's getting closer to Thanksgiving,' Fran reminded. 'These next weeks make or break the year.'

Fran led them to a neighborhood coffee shop – open for dinner but lightly populated thus far. They settled themselves in a booth at the rear, ordered.

'If they didn't have low-fat muffins, I wouldn't have brought you here,' Fran joshed, sighed. 'I look at the figures on the regular muffins – and oh, they're good – but anywhere from eighteen to twenty-two grams of fat. Even I consider that.' Fran paused, her gaze quizzical. 'So what happened today?

Claudia reported on the day's activities. 'Michael may have just been diplomatic when he called me his "new assistant",' she admitted. 'He wouldn't want to say he'd pulled me off the selling floor for two weeks.'

'I'm impressed.' Fran glowed. 'You could be on your way to a permanent job.'

'I know enough not to count on that. And, meanwhile, I've got this problem with Larry.' She explained his phone call in the afternoon. 'Poor kid, he'll be coming to me for the Thanksgiving and Christmas breaks. He'll have to sleep on Laura's convertible sofa.' She grimaced in anticipation.

'Don't knock it,' Fran scolded. 'You know how many people in this country sleep on convertible sofas? When I was growing up in the Bronx, we had a two-bedroom apartment. My parents slept in one bedroom, my two brothers in the other. Baby sister slept on the convertible sofa – until my two brothers were out of college and decided it was time to find an apartment for themselves and I inherited their bedroom.'

'I was an only child – so was Todd. I always wanted a sister or brother,' Claudia reminisced. 'I was so envious of big families.'

'I used to dream of being an only child,' Fran confessed. 'No fights with my brothers – my own bedroom. That was a big day when they moved – for the three of us. It was a Major Step – to move into your own flat. In Manhattan. There was a kind of sophistication about living here.'

'When we moved to New York, I had a sense of setting down roots.' Claudia was somber in recall. 'Now I don't know where I'll be living in three months.'

Claudia ignored dinner, settled for an apple and peppermint tea while she watched the ubiquitous *Law & Order* on television. All across America, she mused, single people – and sometimes couples – ate from TV trays and watched the TV screen.

But her mind strayed from this diversion. When would Larry call? He must understand that he was not to drop out of college. *Somehow, we'll manage.*

She remembered trying to console Mattie when her oldest dropped out of high school last year. She remembered Mattie's heartbreak.

'What chance has that boy got to get a life for himself – out of the projects and bad friends – if he don't have a high school diploma?'

She'd prodded Todd into getting Mattie's son a job in the carpet shop where they'd bought the wall-to-wall carpeting for the condo. And he was doing well until the store closed, and he started hanging out with a neighborhood gang. He'd been working on his high school equivalency test until his dropout friends derided this. Now he was serving time at Riker's Island.

Somehow, she must keep Larry in school. He was super-bright – with a great future ahead, if he didn't allow himself to become sidetracked. All right, so his father was out of their lives. Other single mothers saw their kids through school. A mother's responsibility didn't cease when her children reached eighteen.

Sixteen

'Larry, I won't have you dropping out of school,' Claudia reiterated for the dozenth time. *He's nineteen years old – I won't let that happen.* 'That college degree is essential in this century.' Mattie had bemoaned the lack of vocational training in the school system, she remembered. *'Not every kid has to go to college. Why can't we have schools to train those kids to be electricians and plumbers and house painters? They make a good livin', raise decent families.'*

'Mom, a lot of guys do all right without a college degree.' Larry brought her back to the moment. Even over the phone she sensed his tension. 'Look at Bill Gates – the richest man in the world. He didn't finish college.' *How many times must he tell me that?*

'It won't be easy, but you'll get your degree. Even go on to a master's. Not everybody is a Bill Gates.' Claudia struggled for calm. 'You've got your bartending job for everyday expenses. I can handle the tuition. You'll find a summer job here in the city. There're college loans. You'll go out into the world prepared.'

'I don't like to see you standing on your feet all day in a department store—'

'I'm not standing on my feet all day,' she reminded. 'I've got this special assignment – and I like being out in the business world.' *He's worried for me – my precious baby.* 'And forty-three isn't exactly decrepit. It's the halfway mark in life.' *Forget that forty was being considered 'over the hill' in the eyes of many employers.*

'Mom, you're a special lady. I love you.'

In an effort to unwind, Claudia made herself a cup of chamomile tea and reached for the current issue of *Vanity Fair* – which always contained an article to grab her attention. Magazine in hand, mug of tea close by, she settled herself on the sofa. When the phone rang at close to 11 p.m., she knew the caller would be Shirley. By now the children were asleep and Shirley was what she called 'a temporarily free woman.'

'How're you doing?' Shirley asked with an air of optimism.

'I'm surviving.' *Okay – I'm living from day to day. Don't most people do that?* 'How're the kids?'

For a few minutes they talked about Annie and Scott, about Bill's problems with kids in his supposedly 'good' school. Then Shirley switched into what Claudia had suspected was on her mind from the minute she'd called.

'What's doing with you and Michael?'

'Nothing's doing with me and Michael,' Claudia protested. 'He's a great boss – for the time left in our arrangement. You're reading too many romance novels.'

'You're fond of him,' Shirley said tenderly. 'Something happens in your voice when you talk about him.'

'He's a – a charismatic man.' Claudia searched for words. 'I hear half the women in the store think he's a younger Harrison Ford.'

'Hey, I'd be happy with the real Harrison Ford,' Shirley drawled. 'In my dreams. But Bill's still my guy. Even though he drives me nuts the way he worries about some of the kids he has to deal with. He's a good guidance counselor – but he can't make up for absentee, career-bent parents. The nice suburban house and the two cars – more when the kids are eligible for driver's licenses – don't fill the bill. Parents have to be on the ball. Jill and Larry are lucky – they have a mother who's always there for them.'

'That's all I need in my life – my kids.' Claudia felt a surge of love. 'So stop this Harlequin romance story about Michael Walsh and me. It's not going to happen.'

Again Claudia arrived at Michael's suite of offices before Dolores. Michael's door was closed. She heard a monotone emerging. Michael was reading to himself the sheaf of notes she'd given him before leaving last evening. He'd told her to leave early yesterday. How late had he stayed?

If she was on the selling floor, she'd be off tomorrow – Saturday. Michael had warned that they'd probably be working. So be it, she thought defensively. She was scheduled for a bonus for working with Michael on this project – that was good.

She settled herself in her cubicle, turned on the computer and the monitor. Michael's final words of yesterday afternoon echoed in her brain:

'Forget the restaurant lunches. Concentrate on the report for the main office.' A hint of exultation in his voice. *'Focus on the revised catalogue layouts, follow with a breakdown of the costs – and advantages – of the day-nursery facilities. Write it up the way you discussed it at our meeting.'*

She mustn't be intimidated by this assignment, she ordered herself. She'd written endless reports for the dozen volunteer organizations with whom she'd worked through the years. She'd even written reports from Todd's notes when he was pressed for time. *I can do this.*

She tried to focus on the task at hand. But memory taunted her. Writing a report for a volunteer organization was an amateur deal. This was a major assignment – it could help seal Michael's position as a kind of Wonder Boy at the Miller's chain.

She heard Dolores arrive twenty minutes later. Then Dolores strolled to her cubicle.

'I told the agency we had to have the photos by ten this

morning,' Dolores said and chuckled. 'That way we can be sure of no delays.'

'Great.' *Dolores is a team player – she doesn't consider me an interfering employee.* 'Did Michael set up an appointment with the catalogue layout people?'

'They'll be here at one o'clock for a working lunch.' Dolores giggled. 'Michael won't be brown-bagging it today. I have orders to send up lunch for five at one fifteen sharp.'

Mid-morning Michael emerged from his office. 'Claudia,' he called. 'We need to talk.'

Her heart began to pound. 'I'll be right there.' *Did I do something wrong?* She hurried into his office – questions darting across her mind.

'We have a problem?' She tried to appear casual.

'Claudia, when I call you into my office it doesn't mean we have a problem,' he clucked, but she felt sympathy in him. He sensed her insecurity – but that didn't bother him. Did it?

'Sit down.' He dropped into one corner of the black leather sofa in his office. 'How would you feel about extending your run as my assistant until the end of the year?'

'I'd like that very much.' *Oh, yes!*

'We've got major work ahead. Expect Don Logan to be unreceptive until he's sure he's milked us dry of ideas.'

'But ultimately he'll accept your decisions,' Claudia concluded.

'I believe so.' Michael frowned in thought. 'It's to his advantage to bring Miller's Manhattan out of the red.'

'He's not doing it – you are.' *I'm speaking my mind again. But Michael's pleased. He's smiling.*

'But he'll feel we've done it under his relentless pushing,' Michael interpreted. 'Both sides benefit.' He hesitated. 'When you have the rough draft done, I'd like to sit down with you and go over important points.'

'Fine.' *He's truly anxious about this report. It means a lot to him. Will he take over this store on a permanent basis – or be sent to another store in the chain that's in trouble?*

'I hate to push you, Claudia, but do you feel you'll have a rough draft by tomorrow evening?'

Claudia nodded. 'I'm sure I'll have it ready then—'

'Then let's schedule an evening session,' he began, then paused, all at once apologetic. 'That'll be Saturday night. Do you have other plans?'

'Nothing important.'

'Would you mind if we made it another dinner meeting?' His voice was casual. His eyes exuded a hungry glow.

I'm not imagining it – he is attracted to me. 'That sounds practical.' *Nothing will happen. We're both adults. We both have other commitments. Maybe under other conditions we could have had something beautiful.*

'Let's make a point of getting out of here by six p.m. We'll have dinner by seven p.m. Bring your rough draft in duplicate. We'll talk about it over dinner, get down to serious business after dinner.'

'That sounds good.' *This is a business meeting. Like last time. We both know that. Nothing else will happen.*

Seventeen

Claudia awoke on Saturday at her usual early hour, with an instant realization that she'd be working with Michael this evening. She was having brunch with Jill tomorrow. Fran had suggested a movie this evening, but she'd explained she was busy – implying with family. Fran would make much of this second session at Michael's apartment.

She'd told Fran about staying on as Michael's assistant until the end of the year. *'Ah, hah! He's moving in fast.'* She'd tried – futilely – to convince Fran that Michael was only interested in what she could contribute business-wise.

She heard the persistent sound of rain hitting the windows.

Oddly soothing. Cozy heat rose from the radiators. She was conscious of a sense of sybaritic luxury. A brief escape from the real world.

But in moments reality invaded her. Had she convinced Larry that he must stay in school? That, somehow, they'd see him through to his degree? He was still numbed by the change in their lifestyle. His home was reduced to a convertible sofa in a brief sublet.

I'll be firm. I'll make him understand how important a college degree is in today's job market. He's nineteen years old. What kind of a job could he find if he left school? Working in a fast-food chain? Being a messenger?

She ordered herself to dismiss painful conjecture, try to unwind. Stay in bed a little longer this morning. She'd be working late with Michael, she assuaged a trickle of guilt. Dolores came in around 10:30 on Saturdays, declaring that to sleep later two mornings a week was a deserved luxury.

This morning Chris Taylor was scheduled to move into Jill's apartment. Could that work out? Please, God, don't let that backfire. Had Jill given it serious thought? She could be so impulsive. A talent, Todd had said derisively, that she'd inherited from her mother.

Was it because of the rent situation that she was feeling occasional indications that Jill was becoming disenchanted with her job? For a young woman approaching her twenty-second birthday the salary seemed fantastic – but the hours Jill put in at the company equaled the average two jobs.

'Mom, you don't understand. They have a weeding-out process. They hire a bunch of supposedly bright recent college grads, work them like hell for two years. Then they dump most of them – and push up the few that made it fast. I think I can make the survivors list. It's rough – but it's a great opportunity.'

But a suspicion that Jill was viewing her job with less enthusiasm persisted. Claudia's mind darted back through the years. Jill had gone through the usual teenage madness.

Her sophomore year in high school Jill had vowed she'd be

a rock star. The next year she wanted to be an astronaut. It was Todd who'd turned her on to the systems analyst deal when she was making out college applications.

I just want the kids to be financially secure and happy in their jobs. What most parents want. But isn't it an accepted fact that most people spend their lives in jobs they barely tolerate – or even loathe?

Despite her determination to arrive at the office much later than usual, Claudia was at the store minutes before 9 a.m. The personnel floor was Saturday-quiet. Desks unattended. She walked into Michael's suite with instant knowledge that he was at work. She could hear him pacing about his inner office while he carried on a phone conversation.

She settled herself at her computer. The report was becoming more complicated, she thought uneasily as she settled down to work. At intervals she feared that Michael expected more than she could provide.

She heard the door to Michael's office open. Mug of coffee in hand, he strode out to greet her.

'Repercussions already,' he reported. 'I just got off with somebody from the Chicago office.' Unexpectedly he chuckled. 'And remember the time difference – but he said he's been at his desk for over an hour. My mole,' he explained.

'That's useful.' Claudia waited for him to continue.

'He tells me that Don Logan is pissed about our day-nursery proposal. He figures when we talk about a new project for the entire chain, I'm imposing on his territory.' Michael shrugged. 'So in our report stress we're speaking only for Miller's Manhattan.'

'And Miller's White Plains?' *I'm talking too much again. But Michael's smiling. He approves.*

'Right.' He exuded a glow of satisfaction. 'And by extending it to a second store – though one in my territory – the inference will be that it would be good for all the stores. Work it up in rough – we'll smooth out the rough edges this evening.' For an instant the atmosphere was charged. The glint of anticipation in his eyes more personal than business.

86

Cool it, Claudia. You're seeing what you want to see. For Michael this whole deal is to further his career.

Jill zipped up her jeans, reached for a red turtleneck. On Saturdays informal dress was acceptable. Pulling the turtleneck into place she checked the clock. Where the hell was Chris? She'd told him to be here no later than ten this morning.

The sharp ring of the intercom was jarring. That would be Chris. She hurried into the living room to respond.

'Yes?' she asked, conscious that her voice was terse. *I can handle this scene. We'll barely see each other.*

'Chris is here,' the doorman reported.

'Send him up, José.'

She glanced about the living room and dining area. Fairly decent. Chris wouldn't have to worry about linens, towels. Sandy – feeling some guilt for walking out on such short notice – had left them for her replacement.

Waiting impatiently for Chris to arrive, she brought her L.L.Bean jacket from the hall closet, collected her purse from the coffee table. Theresa was cool. She wouldn't have sent Chris to share if she didn't think it would work out okay.

She heard the elevator pull to a stop on their floor. The door slid open. She reached to open the apartment door. A tall-ish, slim man in jeans and a jacket similar to her own was searching for an apartment number. In addition to a backpack he carried a loaded knapsack.

'Chris?'

'Yeah.' His face lighted. She might be nearsighted, she acknowledged, but she could see that Chris was good looking. So many gay guys were gorgeous. And warm and talented. 'Jill?'

'Right.'

'I have to leave for work,' Jill told him as he approached. 'I've left keys for you – they're on the dresser in your room. If you haven't had breakfast yet, check the fridge. I left the coffee maker on – there're a couple of cups in the carafe. It was just made half an hour ago.' *He's good looking, has a great smile – pity he's gay. Not that I have time to play – not in my job.*

'Hey, that's great.' He deposited the knapsack on the floor, reached to remove the backpack. 'Thanks for taking me in. I was growing desperate.'

'See you later—' She gestured vaguely. *It seems weird – leaving a guy I've just met alone in my apartment.* 'My hours are a little crazy.' She reached for her jacket and purse. *Mom worries he won't be able to afford the rent – but from what Sandy said, he should be able to swing it for a few months.* 'Sometimes I don't get home until three a.m.'

'That's rough.' He moved to open the door for her. 'I hope you take a car service.'

'Oh, sure.' *Wow, he just oozes charm.* 'See you.'

Downstairs Jill searched the street for an empty cab. There, just ahead. She lifted a hand, signaled impatiently. Chris Taylor seemed a great guy. He was Teresa's brother.

It isn't like I'm taking in a stranger.

Eighteen

Claudia discarded endless first pages of the report in work. It must be right. Logan would be looking for holes. But she and Michael would rework it tonight, she reminded herself. What she was doing was only a rough draft.

At truant intervals her mind wandered off to dissect Larry's reaction to her insistence he remain at school. This wasn't the time for him to rebel. At other moments she probed Jill's decision to take in Theresa's brother. Was that a bright idea?

'Coffee?' She was startled by Michael's appearance. 'I

figured this was a time for "the real thing."' He extended one of the pair of oversized mugs he kept in his office.

'Oh, that's great—' She reached out for the mug. 'And you're right – this is not a "decaf" moment.'

Michael returned to his office. Claudia focused on her computer. Be precise in all the costs, she ordered herself as she struggled to present the nursery project in a favorable light – but highlight the advantages. The bottom line, as Michael had pointed out, was to utilize the nursery in heavy sales periods.

Caught up now in completing the report by 6 p.m. – when Michael had suggested they transfer themselves to his apartment, Claudia lost sight of time.

'Would you settle for a roast turkey sandwich on rye toast for lunch?' Again Michael's presence startled her.

'That would be great—' Only now did she realize she was hungry.

'I'll call the Oasis, have sandwiches sent up,' he said briskly and took off.

The rest of the day fled past. As anticipated, the catalogue crew arrived early afternoon, and remained for two hours of electric discussion. At a few moments before 6 p.m. Michael closed up his office and ordered Claudia to join him. She piled the pages of the report into an envelope, reached for her coat and purse. She'd read and reread, made endless revisions on the report. Would Michael be satisfied with it?

'I know it's selfish of me to demand your time on a Saturday evening,' he apologized while they headed for the elevator.

'I don't mind. I had nothing special planned.' *Why did I say that? It sounds as though I'd just be sitting at home, having dinner on a tray before the TV set. But I would be.*

They hurried from the store and out into the night. The temperature had dropped since morning. A sharp wind intensified the drop.

'We'll grab a cab—' Michael guided her towards the curb, an arm raised as a cab turned into the avenue.

'This is luck on a Saturday night at this hour,' he commented, pulling the cab door open for her.

While the cab zigzagged through early evening traffic, Michael talked about a phone session he'd had with co-workers at the White Plains store.

'The feedback was good,' he said with satisfaction. 'While we have no approval yet, they've figured out the space we'd need for the nursery project. And, of course, the White Plains store will receive the same catalogues as Miller's Manhattan.'

The cab pulled up before Michael's apartment house. What a blustery evening, Claudia thought as they emerged from the warmth of the cab and darted towards the entrance.

'No crockpot in work today.' Michael's smile was wry. 'I fell out of bed, grabbed breakfast and headed for the office.'

'We can order in—' Claudia's voice was sympathetic.

Michael grimaced in rejection. 'I'll dig up something. I have chicken cutlets and—' He frowned in thought. 'Maybe we'll have to stop and shop.'

'Do you have pasta?' she asked on impulse while they headed for the elevator.

'Always.' He waited for her to continue. 'The wholewheat blend kind.'

'What other would you have?' She laughed, feeling strangely secure with him on these grounds. Away from the office he seemed another person. 'You have a food processor,' she recalled. 'Let me throw together a "quickie" dinner my kids have always liked on a cold, blustery night like this. Spaghetti and meatballs.' She chuckled at his look of surprise. She'd mentioned at their last dinner that she never ate beef. 'I use chicken. I'll need breadcrumbs and—'

'I have breadcrumbs – the kind with Italian season—' He paused, his smile apologetic. 'They do it so well, why should I?'

'Right.' In this kind of camaraderie, she thought, she'd approve anything he said. Later – after dinner – they'd return to their business roles.

They walked into an empty elevator. Michael pushed the button for his floor – inadvertently brushing her shoulder in the effort. She felt a sudden touch of arousal. *Why am I reacting this way? It's insane.*

'What else will you need?' It was as though he'd cleared his mind of everything except dinner, Claudia thought.

'One egg – and I don't use all the yolk. Just a bit.' He was tuned in – as she was – to the value of a health-guided diet. 'And some fresh herbs—' *Perhaps we should have stopped to shop.*

'I have my herb pots,' he reminded in triumph. 'Take your pick. And I always have salad makings in the house. And made-from-scratch tomato sauce in the freezer. Hey, we're in business.'

Michael unlocked the apartment door, threw it wide with an air of moving into another world. 'I'll put some music on the CD player.' He stopped short. 'Damn, the chicken cutlets are frozen.'

'They won't be after a few minutes under running hot water.' She pulled off her coat, gave it to Michael to hang away. 'I know the way to the kitchen,' she tossed off lightly. *Why is it when I walk into Michael's apartment I feel as though I've been reborn – a new person?*

She stood before the opened freezer while the exquisite strains of Tchaikovsky's *Swan Lake* filtered into the room. Here were chicken cutlets. Put them under hot running water to defrost. *Why do I feel so relaxed, so at peace when I'm here this way? As though I belong here.*

'What can I do to help?' Michael stood in the doorway of the kitchen.

'Dice an onion. Bring out the breadcrumbs. Crack an egg, remove most of the yolk, then beat it,' Claudia instructed while she filled a pot with cold water and placed it on a gas burner. 'Oh, you wouldn't have a grinder?' She had expected to use the food processor that sat on the counter, but a grinder would be better.

'Of course I have a grinder,' he chided good-humoredly, and reached into a cabinet to bring it down. 'Now to the onion, the egg, and the breadcrumbs – and the wholewheat blend

91

pasta.' He reached into the cabinet again, then moved to the refrigerator.

Claudia read the directions on the box of pasta. 'Let's get the pasta up, then start the grill for the chicken. Timing must be just right.'

For no reason that Claudia could understand Michael lost his air of levity. 'Sometimes I think timing is the most important ingredient in life.' His eyes clung to hers. *He's saying the timing for us is bad.* 'I wish we'd met fifteen years ago.'

'Yes,' she whispered. Heart pounding. Fifteen years ago she'd known her marriage was a sham.

'Think of all the great meals we could have concocted.' He brushed aside the charged moment.

'Thousands,' she declared, simultaneously relieved and disappointed that he'd banished the electric connection between them.

He stood still – listening to the music. 'Do you like ballet?'

'I love it.' Here was a safe subject. She'd attended performances in season when Todd was out of town. He'd loathed ballet. 'I haven't been this season,' she confessed, 'but I never miss a performance of ice-skating on TV – and some of the top skaters are like ballet dancers on ice. I know,' she conceded, 'you're supposed to call it figure skating.' *Why is Michael staring at me that way?*

'You're an ice-skating buff,' he said with a glow of pleasure. 'I fell in love with ice-skating twenty years ago. The great skaters are like poetry on ice,' he murmured with awe. 'That's the only thing that can pull me away from the office on Saturdays – an afternoon telecast of a competition or an exhibition.'

'I remember when my kids were little,' Claudia reminisced. 'Larry was seven, Jill was nine. We were in New York for a visit around Christmas time – and I took them to see *The Nutcracker*. Larry was fascinated – he immediately insisted on taking ballet lessons.' Tender laughter lit her eyes. 'Then his friends at school found out and began to tease him. He dropped it fast. Now he's a sophomore at college and not sure what he wants to do with his life.'

'Your daughter?' Michael asked while they worked in silent communication. *He's not just making conversation – he's truly interested.*

'She went straight from school to a brokerage firm – as a systems analyst.' Claudia frowned. 'I have this uneasy feeling that she's becoming disenchanted with the job. The hours are insane—' *Why did I say that again? He works insane hours.*

All at once Michael was somber. 'Insane hours are fine when you're working at something you love.'

'You love what you're doing,' she said gently.

'No,' he rejected with a violence that startled her. 'I tell myself it's a challenge – that I could never resist a challenge. But I work to build up the figures on my paycheck. So I can meet my obligations with less pain.' He was silent for a moment, seeming caught up in recall. 'I've told you about my ex-wife. She's a semi-invalid – the result of her pregnancy.' He hesitated, seeming in some inner turmoil. 'She has a condo in Scottsdale, is in and out of the Mayo Clinic there.' He shuddered. 'With no health insurance. The bills are staggering.'

'That's rough.'

'A string of doctors were convinced her illness was psychosomatic. But a psychosomatic patient may imagine pain – but feels it.' His face tightened. 'It's my responsibility to care for her needs. A very expensive responsibility.'

He's so ethical. So compassionate. Everything that Todd wasn't.

'Why couldn't we have met fifteen years ago?'

He's telling me he feels something special for me – as I do for him. But there's this ex-wife who controls his life. Why couldn't we have met back in college – before I knew Todd, before he met his ex-wife?

Our timing is wrong.

Nineteen

The phone rang – shattering the confessional moment between them. Michael swore under his breath, reached for the kitchen extension.

'Yes.' Impersonal but polite. He frowned. 'We're in the middle of dinner. Sorry.' He put down the phone with a grunt of impatience. 'Why do telecommunications people always call when you're preparing dinner or eating it? Wasn't there some law just passed to keep them from intruding this way?'

'I gather there're a lot of exceptions.' Relieved yet disappointed at this intrusion, she focused on grinding the chicken. Michael was busy at the herb pots. *He's regretting what he almost said to me. He's always so in control – I'm usually the outspoken person.*

They concentrated on teamwork in preparing their dinner. It was though, Claudia thought, they'd arrived at an unspoken decision to shelve their personal emotions. *This is a business meeting. We have a report to finish.*

While they worked together to get dinner on the table, Michael talked abut his fascination with cooking and the restaurant business. A safe topic of conversation.

'We're the minority, you know.' She sighed as they settled themselves at the dining table. 'How many people are serious about nutrition, about avoiding obesity?'

'More than you think,' he insisted. 'In the grocery stores, supermarkets, people are reading labels. The few health-food restaurants are doing well. Even some of the fast-food chains are latching on to this trend.' He dug into his salad with approval. The dressing spontaneously concocted by Claudia at the last moment. 'You've got to write down the recipe for this dressing. It's super – and guilt free.'

They lingered over what Michael called his semi-guilt-free dessert.

'When I'm especially uptight, I bake,' he confided. 'I defrosted a mini carrot cake this morning.'

'Semi-guilt-free?' Claudia was good-humoredly skeptical. But they were on safe ground. 'Tell me, what goes in it?'

'I use just a tiny bit of oil,' he began.

'In carrot cake?' She shook her head in disbelief. 'Every cookbook I've ever read calls for at least a cup of oil.'

'I use – in the batter for a regular-sized cake, which I divide into minis – only a tablespoon,' he said in triumph. 'And I—'

'Use apple sauce to make up for the rest,' Claudia realized – her own substitution for oil. 'And raisins and crushed pineapple – with only one whole egg and the rest just egg whites,' she added.

'And a few walnuts – very healthful,' he reminded.

'For a frosting you used low-fat cream cheese,' she guessed.

He beamed. 'Right on target. The fat-free didn't make it—' For a heated moment their eyes clung – saying what they didn't dare allow themselves to voice. 'I'll get our coffee—' He broke the spell.

He wants to make love to me – I know that. And if he tries, I won't stop him.

Michael returned with their coffee. Immediately he launched into the business at hand. Not trusting himself away from that cover, Claudia taunted herself. *All right, you're here to finalize the report. Concentrate on business. No room in Michael's life for anything else.*

They were both blessed with the ability to block out of their minds everything but the task at hand, Claudia recognized as they dug into the project at hand. Yet at truant moments other emotions intruded – and she sensed that Michael, too, was conscious of these aberrant moments.

Earlier than she'd anticipated – it was barely 10 p.m., she noted – Michael declared the report in shape to present to Don Logan. 'I'll fax it tomorrow morning.' *He's going in to the office tomorrow – but he didn't ask me to come in.* 'Don will have it on his desk when he arrives Monday morning.'

'He can't expect better than that.' *Don Logan won't be in his office on a weekend.*

'I'll go down with you and put you into a taxi.' He was at the guest closet to retrieve her coat. 'Sometimes it's hard to find one on a Saturday evening.' His eyes were opaque now. *What is he thinking?*

'You don't need to do that. The rush comes when the theaters let out.' *Why do I feel this way? As though I'll die if he doesn't make love to me.*

'I want to do it.' He was brusque.

He held her coat for her – and suddenly she was in his arms. His mouth on hers. Her arms tightened about his shoulders. *Oh, this is good. This is so right.* Then all at once he was releasing her. *Why?*

'I'm sorry.' His voice was anguished. 'I had no right to do that—'

'Why not?' she challenged – astonishing herself. *This is so right.* 'We're both free.' She would be – in a matter of days.

'I'm not.' He closed his eyes for an instant. 'I'm not a free man, Claudia. I have obligations.' His face tightened. 'The divorce settlement includes a clause that says I must cover all of Lisa's living expenses until her health is normal – and she has no health insurance,' he added heavily. 'There's no room in my life for anything else.'

She hesitated, trembling. 'We'll forget it happened,' she said unsteadily. *How can I forget it?*

'Yes,' he agreed, exuding an air of relief.

I'm not being fired. He doesn't want to banish me from his life. Not until the first of the year.

'You're a very special lady,' he murmured while she slid into her coat.

For a wistful instant she felt that he was about to pull her into his arms again. But that moment was over.

Claudia dealt with the two locks on her apartment door, walked inside, hung away her coat. Michael had been so sweet, insisting on putting her into a cab, reminding her to ask for a receipt for her expense account. But why did he feel this overwhelming obligation to an ex-wife?

She sat at a corner of the sofa – in the soft illumination of one lamp – and considered this. It was the question of money, wasn't it? Michael led an austere life financially because of *her* demands.

But why can't we have a relationship? Why deny ourselves something so beautiful? So perfect? This is the twenty-first century. Men and woman have relationships – no ties, no demands. How can I make Michael understand that?

Jill and Larry would be so shocked – but didn't the young go into relationships without remorse? Probably Larry would be most shocked, she considered tenderly. It would be difficult for him to envision his mother having an affair.

She glanced at her watch. Shirley would have put the kids to bed. Bill would be surfing the TV for something he considered relaxing. Call Shirley.

Shirley picked up on the first ring. 'Hello.'

'I had a working dinner with Michael,' Claudia began.

'Again?' Shirley chortled. 'You're moving fast.'

'There's a huge obstacle,' Claudia said. 'His ex-wife.'

'Tell me how an ex-wife can be an obstacle.'

Claudia reported on the encounter with Michael. 'I can't believe myself,' she confessed. 'I wanted him to make love to me. It's been so long – so many years – since I've felt this way. With Todd it meant nothing after those first few years. For him it was just a quick physical relief. I might have been some call girl – except that he didn't have to pay me.'

'A lot of women put up with that,' Shirley said. 'Accept it as a business arrangement. My neighbor across the road told me just last week, "If Joe is running around with other women, I don't want to know about it." For some women marriage is a job. They're taken care of – the kids needs are provided. They don't want to lose the job – even if it means looking the other way.'

'I'm out of my mind to allow myself to become emotionally involved,' Claudia said in sharp self-reproach. 'I've seen other divorced women make asses of themselves over a man. That won't be me.'

'Honey, give yourself a break. This Michael Walsh sounds like somebody fine. So you struck out with Todd. Don't rule this one out. You're a young woman!'

'In a few weeks I'll be out of a job. Out of an apartment. And I've got Larry to think about. Somehow, I've got to manage to see him through the next two years of college. Why am I behaving like a love-starved teenager? It's time I got my priorities straight.'

Twenty

In the midst of a chaotic dream – in the cozy warmth of her bedroom – Jill was awakened by the shrill intrusion of the alarm clock. Without opening her eyes she reached over to silence the monster on the night table beside her bed. Realizing it must be 10 a.m. – and she had a brunch appointment with her mother at 11.

What time had she called the car service last night to bring her home from the office? It was past 2 a.m., she recalled with a sense of outrage. A hell of a way to spend a Saturday evening! Not what she'd anticipated when she took the job.

Dad was such a bastard, she thought with recurrent frustration. How could he treat Mom that way? Not just the divorce bit – but leaving her broke. She'd been furious with him since the time she saw him with that woman. Why hadn't she told Mom then? If Mom had divorced him before this craziness with the company, she could have come out with a decent settlement.

The situation was rough on Larry, too – with two years of college ahead of him. Could he pick up enough loans to see him through? *Will I be able to help, now that Chris is sharing the rent? Mom's nervous this will be a short-term arrangement.*

She pulled herself into a semi-sitting position, strained for sounds in other areas of the apartment. Was Chris still asleep – or had he gone out already? His bedroom door was closed when she got home last night – no sounds from his room.

She tossed aside the comforter, geared herself to shower. Where was she meeting Mom? The Lyric, she remembered – a quick walk from Mom's apartment. Mom's apartment for another few weeks, she thought uneasily. Everything was so uncertain. They were living from day to day. *How the hell did I convince myself this would be a great job? I hate it.*

Conscious of the time, she spent only a few minutes in the shower, emerged to dress. Jeans, a sweatshirt, New Balance. Only a quick touch of lipstick. She flipped on her bedroom computer to check on the weather. Cold and cloudy. She reached into the room-wide closet of her bedroom for her L.L.Bean jacket – her day off from work uniform.

She collected her shoulder bag, left her bedroom. She was aware of the fragrant aroma of freshly brewed coffee, went into the galley kitchen. A carafe of coffee sat on the coffee maker, a note beside it.

Hi – It's a little past 9:30 – so if you're up within an hour the coffee should be okay. On my budget this is a better deal than Starbucks! Have a great day. Chris.

Jill poured coffee into a mug, drank it quickly and with appreciation. A good omen, she told herself, put the mug into the dishwasher. All right, get this show on the road.

She left the house, grabbed a cab to Third Avenue and 22nd Street. Walking into the Lyric – bustling at this hour – she spied her mother sitting in a booth at the far side of the restaurant. She glanced at her watch in sudden guilt. No, it was barely 11. Leave it to Mom to be early.

'Hi, darling.' Claudia glanced up with a welcoming smile. Unlike Todd – who was always late for appointments – the kids could tell time, she told herself with approval. 'Does this feel like dawn to you?'

'I was in bed before midnight,' Jill lied. 'Slept straight through. Crazy dreams.' She grimaced in recall.

'How's the roommate situation?' Claudia strived to appear casual.

'Chris moved in yesterday. I saw him just a bit – I was on my way to the office. I guess he left early today – there was brewed coffee waiting for me.'

A friendly bus boy appeared with a carafe of coffee, refilled Claudia's cup, then returned with a cup for Jill.

'What're you having?' Jill asked. She glanced at the menu.

'Orange juice and wholewheat pancakes. They're great,' Claudia told her.

'I'll have the same.' Jill discarded the menu. 'How's the job?'

She's still worrying about me?

'You're still on that special assignment?'

'Until the first of the year,' Claudia reminded. She'd played down her part in Michael's campaign, indicated she was involved in basic office routine. *Is Jill afraid I'll be fired even from this temporary job? It's hard for the kids to visualize me as a working woman. It's so sweet – the way they worry about me.*

She'd been deliberate about not mentioning the two meetings at Michael's apartment. She could envision Jill's reaction.

'Mom, he's out to drag you into bed. Don't let him take advantage of you.'

While Jill digressed into minor company gossip, Claudia remembered three occasions when a business associate of Todd's had made a play for her – and Todd had urged her to play along.

'He controls a massive amount of business. I'm not suggesting you hop into bed with the horny bastard – just kid him along until I have a deal sewed up.'

She'd been shocked and furious until another wife had made it clear this was simply part of the job of being a corporate wife.

'Mom, you're not with me,' Jill scolded, bringing her back to the moment.

'I'm sorry, darling – I just remembered something I should do at the office in the morning,' she fabricated.

'You're taking this job seriously.' Surprise blended with respect in Jill's voice.

'Of course I do.' A hint of reproach in Claudia's voice. Hadn't she always told the kids, 'Whatever you do, give it your best.'

'Well, at least you don't work the crazy hours I do.'

Jill sees me on a routine schedule – but I'm getting overtime plus a bonus. To move up, people work extra hours.

'I know,' Jill was almost defensive now, 'if I can make the cut, move up at the end of another year, I'll be pulling in a fabulous salary.'

But she doesn't seem enthralled at the prospect. 'Honey, are you burned out on this job?' Claudia tried to be casual.

Jill was startled. 'I didn't say that—'

'But it sneaks through—'

'I can't afford to be burned out.'

Claudia felt her tension.

'I have a two-year lease on a ghastly high rental. And with so many jobs going overseas—' Her frown was eloquent.

'What would you like to be doing?' *This a dangerous path – I'm talking too much again.*

Their waitress appeared. For a few moments they focused on ordering. Now they were alone again. Claudia pursued her earlier conversation. 'Jill, what would you like to be doing?'

'Oh, it's crazy.' Jill dismissed this, but the glint in her eyes captured Claudia's attention.

'I went through your rock star stage and the wanna-be astronaut scene,' Claudia tried for humor. 'I think I can handle whatever you have in mind.'

'Remember Diane Miller? I brought her home with me one Thanksgiving weekend in our junior year.'

'Oh, I liked Diane. She was bright, articulate. She truly had her feet on the ground,' Claudia recalled.

'Diane needed that – considering what her parents are like.' Jill exuded contempt.

'Right,' Claudia concurred with sympathy. Diane had had an emergency appendectomy the Sunday before Thanksgiving

– and her mother and father had flown down to Palm Beach for a week, leaving her in the hospital. She'd been dismissed on the Wednesday before the holiday, and Jill had called home to say she was bringing Diane with her. 'But what about Diane?'

'She and her boyfriend – they'll probably get married when they find time – are working their butts off in this publicity firm they've set up. They're not making much money yet – but they're making real headway.' Jill glowed. 'It's a fascinating field. I know,' she kidded, 'it's not like joining the Peace Corps or working for the environment – but I listen to Diane and Zach, and I feel like I'm at the starting gate at the race-track and just waiting for the word to run.'

'When did all this happen?' Claudia was mystified. *All Jill talked about her last year in college was making it with a top firm in the investment banking field – and she was doing that.*

'It's been kind of building up since Diane and Zach opened their office five months ago. But forget it, Mom.' Jill was brusque. 'I'm staying with the company. I'd be a nutcase to give it up now.'

Claudia's mind flashed back in time. Michael, too, seemed at the top of the world – yet he loathed his job. Those in this world who work in fields that they care about are blessed, she thought wistfully. And they are few.

Twenty-One

Along with countless working women, Claudia spent Sunday afternoon in vacuuming, dusting, and mopping the galley-kitchen floor. Activities made less boring by the strains of Tchaikovsky's Symphony No. 5 drifting into the apartment. While she was contemplating dinner – with no enthusiasm - the phone rang.

She reached to pick up. This was her social life, she thought with wry humor.

'Hello.'

'I was thinking,' Shirley began with her usual 'rush to the point' inclination. 'Why don't you invite Michael to dinner at your place? I mean, you've had dinner at his place twice.'

'Business dinners,' Claudia pointed out. 'And last night he made it clear. There's no space in his life for me. For any woman—'

'Something happened last night – more than you're telling me—'

'It was nothing,' Claudia dismissed this. Not even with Shirley could she talk about those brief moments in Michael's arms. 'He said our – our timing was all wrong.'

'He's divorced,' Shirley said bluntly. 'You're almost divorced. What's the problem? Why should an ex-wife stand between you?'

'He has to provide a very expensive lifestyle for his semi-invalid ex-wife.'

'That sounds like something out of a Victorian novel,' Shirley shrugged this off. 'This is the twenty-first century. So you don't jump into marriage again.' Her voice softened. 'A relationship can be very consoling.'

'He might change his mind if he wins a major lottery. And that's not about to happen.' *Move into safer territory.* 'How're the kids?'

'At the moment mortal enemies.' Shirley chuckled. 'But you know the routine. Oh, I want the three of you to come to us for Thanksgiving.'

Claudia was startled. Her mind made swift calculation. 'I can't believe it's barely three weeks away!'

'Take an early train and—'

'Shirley, I think – this first Thanksgiving out of the condo – it might be wiser for me to have Jill and Larry over to dinner in the apartment. You know, sort of reminding the kids we're still a family. Larry will be sleeping there for the long weekend – on the convertible sofa—' Her voice ebbed away.

'He'll survive. Bill slept on a studio couch in the living room until he was fourteen – when the family moved into a larger apartment.'

'The kids are okay,' Claudia said with determined optimism. 'We're not going to fall apart.' She paused. 'Of course, I worry about both of them. Larry having to change schools midway. And I've got a suspicion Jill is losing her enthusiasm for her job.'

'This isn't the time to start looking for another,' Shirley shot back. 'Bill is developing a real hate for his job – but he's not about to try to move on. Not with the mortgage payments, the car loans, the credit card bills – and braces for Annie coming up soon. But right now I'd better start throwing dinner together. If you change your mind about Thanksgiving dinner, remember it's a standing invite. And here's a thought, honey. Why not invite Michael Walsh for Thanksgiving dinner?'

'Shirley, give it up!' But Claudia's laughter was tender.

Off the phone with Shirley, Claudia focused on preparing a quick, simple dinner. But the approaching Thanksgiving lingered in her mind. Instinct told her that Michael would be alone on Thanksgiving.

She remembered the cabinet that held his supply of dinnerware. Only two of everything – and she suspected she was a rare guest in Michael's apartment. *We're living in such an insane world. Why not grab every bit of happiness we can?*

Everybody worried about the dreadful job market – with so many jobs going out of the country. About terrorism – an ever-present threat. About the environment and soaring health insurance premiums and the hidden inflation – where products dropped in weight but not in cost.

She carried her dinner tray into the living room, placed it on a snack table set before the sofa. A daring thought darting across her mind – planted there earlier by Shirley.

Do I dare invite Michael to Thanksgiving dinner? As a friend. Will the kids be annoyed at having a stranger – to them – at the Thanksgiving table?

She'd be very casual about it to Jill and Larry. She might even say that it was a move to extend her job beyond the first of the year. But would Michael accept? She'd wait a few days then – towards the end of the week – invite him to Thanksgiving dinner.

Oh, that's a crazy idea! To invite him to dinner with me and my kids. That makes me appear a conniving woman. He made it clear – there's no room in his life for me.

She reached for the remote, flipped on the TV set. Thousands of other divorced – or single or widowed – women sat alone before a TV set and ate a solitary dinner. It wasn't a catastrophe.

After a night of broken slumber, Claudia came fully awake before her alarm clock thrust her into a new day. She lay back against the pillows and thought about her conversation with Shirley late yesterday afternoon.

'This is the twenty-first century. So you don't jump into marriage again. A relationship can be very consoling.'

She and Michael were 'ships that pass in the night.' Who would be hurt if – in the passage of time allotted them – they had a passionate affair? He was such a warm, tender, compassionate man.

Lying alone in bed – remembering Michael's arms about her, their bodies touching, his mouth on hers – she knew there must be more for them than that brief moment. Just being alone with him was sweet torment. Making love would be heaven.

Oh, what is the matter with me? I'm behaving like a lovesick teenager! It's all part of the divorce syndrome – I'll get over this insanity in time. Won't I?

Twenty-Two

Claudia sighed. This would be a dreary day. No sunlight – only a murky grayness crept between the bedroom drapes. A glance at the clock told her she could linger in the comforting warmth of her bed for another half hour. Yet she was conscious of an impatience to be out of the apartment and en route to the office.

She hadn't seen Michael since Saturday evening. It seemed an eternity. It wasn't love for the job that sent her in to the office early, she taunted herself as she thrust aside the comforter and headed for a shower. Michael drew her to the office.

Her job would end with the dawn of the new year. And she'd never see Michael again. Already she felt a sickening sense of loss. How had this happened so fast?

She prepared for the day with her usual compulsive swiftness, was about to leave the apartment when the phone rang. *Why do I always get this feeling of misgiving when the phone rings these days?* Because, she told herself, only those very close to her had this number.

'Hello.'

'It's me.' Shirley, sounding tense, faintly breathless. 'I was hoping I'd catch you before you left – though I shouldn't dump this on you—'

'Shirl, what's up?' Instantly anxious.

'I just needed to talk to somebody. I know there's nothing you can do—'

'Shirl, what's wrong?'

'Bill went for his annual physical about a week ago. Just routine – we thought. Then this morning Dr Lindsey called. He's at the hospital making rounds by seven a.m., he said.' Shirley took a deep breath. 'He said he didn't like the results from Bill's echocardiogram. He said there're a couple of problems with Bill's heart – he wants him to set up an appointment with a cardiologist.'

'Have him take another test,' Claudia said instantly. Bill with heart problems? It was frightening. 'It may be wrong. That happens—'

'Bill brought that up. Dr Lindsey said he'd had it read by a top cardiologist.'

'There could have been a mistake in the lab.' Terrifying visions darted across her mind. This couldn't be happening to Bill. Working so hard to give his family a good life. Bill, who was forever going out of his way to be helpful to the less fortunate. 'He must take another test – it's important.'

Shirley groaned. 'Our health insurance won't cover it. What do you suppose it would cost?'

'Whatever it costs, make Bill take another test,' Claudia insisted, moving into what Larry called her 'mother takes charge' mode. 'Has he showed any symptoms of a heart problem?'

'No. Nothing—'

'He doesn't smoke, he doesn't drink, he's not an ounce overweight, he works out. Make sure he takes another test,' Claudia reiterated.

'He'll fight it. We're always over-budget. You know how it is with a house – something unexpected always pops up. Like the septic tank backing up last month—'

'Shirl, you can't look at the expense at a time like this.'

'You're right. I'll talk to him,' Shirley agreed after a moment, sighed. 'Now there'll be another agonizing wait till the second test results come through. What a hell of a Thanksgiving this is going to be.'

'Not if the first test proves wrong. It happens even in the best of labs. Remember years ago, when your mother was still living and was scheduled to go in for cataract surgery – and it was held up because of some test she'd taken? And then the doctor told her there'd been a mistake – the report was on somebody else's test – she was fine.'

'Right.' A glint of hope in Shirley's voice now. 'Keep your fingers crossed. I need – the children need Bill. He's forty-four years old – he should have half his life ahead of him.'

107

'Promise me, you'll make Bill take another echocardiogram,' Claudia tried again.

'He'll take it. I'll remind him about Mom. Claudia,' she said tenderly, 'you always come through.'

Off the phone Claudia sat motionless. Shaken by the possibility that Bill – always sturdy as a rock – might have serious heart problems. One day he was fine – now he and Shirley were terrified of what lay ahead.

How dare I wallow in self-pity! I'm healthy – Jill and Larry are healthy. The news is full of tragic events – terrible things happening to good people. But please, God, let Bill be all right.

She ordered herself to head for the office. She made a last-minute decision to take an umbrella. The tiny one that would fit into her purse. Unless there was a real downpour, she'd walk to work.

Claudia exchanged the usual greeting with her doorman, headed out into the street. People were walking fast, she noted – shoulders hunched against the cold. She was glad she'd dressed warmly.

But her thoughts returned to the phone conversation with Shirley. She was so upset. Who wouldn't be, facing a diagnosis like that? It would be awful if Bill was incapacitated. She wouldn't allow herself to think beyond that.

Shirley had little work experience. In today's market where would she find a decent-paying job? They could lose the house. Bill wouldn't even be eligible for unemployment insurance. How would they survive?

Settling herself in her cubicle, Claudia planned her day. For a few days everything had been put on hold to prepare the report – which was waiting now on Don Logan's desk in Chicago. As usual, Michael was at work in his office. She heard him dictating into the machine – which Dolores would transcribe later. Dolores was at her computer. Another day had begun.

At intervals Claudia was assaulted by recall of those heated moments in Michael's apartment. He'd been so self-chastising. *'I'm not a free man, Claudia. I have obligations.'* He'd seemed so relieved when she'd said, 'We'll forget it happened.' But she couldn't forget.

Michael stayed closeted in his office. His lunch arrived on a tray from the Oasis. No brown-bagging today. She'd gone down to pick up a container of low-fat yogurt for her own lunch. Dolores took the tray from the Oasis in to Michael's office, emerged with a frown.

'He's so uptight,' Dolores whispered to her. 'The call from Don Logan,' she guessed. 'That man is such a creep.'

But that man had tremendous power in the corporation, Claudia thought uneasily. Was he displeased with their report? She searched her mind for a reason for Logan to have rejected the report. It was good, she told herself – offering innovative suggestions for bringing in shoppers.

In the middle of the afternoon Michael opened his door, yelled to Claudia to come into his office. Michael never yelled at her. He never yelled at anybody. Oh yes, he was upset.

'I had a call from Don Logan,' he told her when she was seated in his office while he paced. 'He's such a bastard. I – we – played down the bit about these proposals being ideal for the entire chain – but he feels threatened. He's asking all kinds of questions. Let's figure out the diplomatic answers.'

They tossed ideas back and forth without arriving at what they felt would pacify Logan.

'I have a mole in the Chicago office,' Michael reminded her.

'Any clue about why Logan is being so negative?' Claudia asked.

'Logan's pissed because he's afraid he'll be outranked if I keep moving along these lines.' Michael abandoned his compulsive pacing, sat down. 'Oh Lord, it's past six! We've been at this almost three hours.' He hesitated. 'You game for more of the same?'

'Yes.' *Is he going to suggest dinner at his apartment again? That always seems to give him a second wind.*

'The Oasis is open till seven tonight,' he said after a moment. 'I'll call down for turkey sandwiches and coffee. Okay?'

'Sure.' *He thought about their working at his apartment and discarded it. He didn't trust himself.*

Dolores had left for the day. Michael made the call to the restaurant himself. He seemed to be involved in some mental struggle.

'The mole told me something else.' He was making an effort to appear casual – but his eyes sent a different message. 'The main office is considering sending me out to Los Angeles to deal with that store. It's in bad shape. Provided I bring Miller's Manhattan up to scratch.'

'You will.' She managed to sound convincing. *If he goes out to Los Angeles, I'll never see him again.*

'Okay.' Michael began to pace again. 'Let's come up with some irrefutable answers for this sonofabitch.'

He doesn't want to go out to Los Angeles, Claudia told herself in shaky triumph. If he returned to the White Plains store, they'd be able to see each other. His eyes told her he ached to make love to her right now.

Why couldn't he seize the moment? Live for today. Why rob themselves of what could be theirs? *So we can't have the whole cake. I'll settle for crumbs.*

Twenty-Three

Close to 9 p.m. Michael declared they'd gone as far as they could on the report.

'I've been as diplomatic as I can,' he told Claudia. 'Make the changes on the computer tomorrow morning. I'll fax it to Logan as soon as you're done.'

'Right.'

'Let's get out of here. I'll put you in a cab.' He paused. 'To hell with this cab business in the future.'

Another few weeks?

'In the morning tell Dolores to open an account for us with a car service.'

Both of them exhausted from the long, troublesome day, they were silent as they headed for the elevator. Just outside the store Michael spied a cab approaching, whistled.

'See you in the morning,' he said briskly as the cab pulled to a stop at the curb. 'Remember to get a receipt for your expense account. And get a good night's sleep.' For an instant – as she stepped into the cab – his eyes rested on her with a glow that sent her heart racing. Then he was closing the cab door and striding northward.

With the light evening traffic she was home in a few minutes. She'd call Shirley, she told herself as she unlocked her apartment door. The flashing light on the answering machine told her there was a message. She pushed the 'play' button and Shirley's voice drifted into the room:

'Hi, I talked to Bill the way you said – and he's scheduling another test. Pray the first one is wrong! No need to call back, honey.'

Thank God for that, Claudia told herself. But Shirl would be a nervous wreck until the results of the second test came through. One day the world looks fine – and the next day disaster can hit. But the kids and she were all right – they'd survive the craziness with Todd.

She was tired – but too wired to sleep. She'd bake, she decided on impulse. Those little fruit squares the kids always liked. Take half a dozen of them to the store – for Dolores and Michael and herself. They could have them at their coffee break. Dolores was forever talking about dieting – but they were low-fat.

She always relaxed when she baked. Michael had said something about relaxing when he cooked. *We're alike in so many ways. We belong together.*

*   *   *

111

Jill frowned in sleep. Aware of disturbing sounds. Then a woman screamed, and she was fully awake. The sounds were coming from the apartment just above hers. Furniture was being thrown about. A man was shouting in rage. Jill's gaze swung to the clock on her chest of drawers. It was 5:18 a.m. What was going on up there?

It was the apartment of what she suspected was a high-priced call girl. Limos appeared at intervals, to disgorge middle-aged men in two-thousand-dollar suits. Sometimes a recognizable celebrity.

Instinctively – in her ballerina-length nightie – she hurried out into the living room to buzz the doorman. Chris was emerging from his room – in the jockey shorts that were ostensibly his nightwear.

'What the hell's going on up there?' Chris demanded while Jill buzzed the doorman.

'José, the woman above me is being beat up!'

'I can't leave the door.' José's voice said he didn't want to become involved. 'Call the police.'

Now the terrified screams of a very young child pierced the night.

'That's her little boy—'

'I'm going up there—' Chris was charging back into his bedroom. 'Call 911.'

Jill rushed to the phone, punched in the numbers, explained the situation. Chris hurried out of his room, zipping his slacks as he headed for the door. Sneakers untied.

'Chris, don't go up there,' Jill warned in alarm. 'You could get hurt.'

'There's a little kid up there. He's scared to death – watching his mother being beat up—' Chris pulled the door wide.

'Chris, be careful—' But he was already out the door and headed for the stairs. She listened – anxious for Chris's well-being – to the heated voices upstairs now. A man – and Chris. The little boy – Jill remembered seeing the toddler with his mother in the elevator – crying piteously.

Other sounds now. The police had arrived, she realized in

relief. She waited for Chris to return. What was happening up there?

Did Theresa lie to me about her brother being gay? Chris's reaction to what happened upstairs was very macho.

The door swung open. Only now did she realize she hadn't bothered to lock it when Chris dashed out that way. Chris strode into the living room with a glow of satisfaction.

'The cops threw him out – with his luggage,' Chris reported and grinned. 'Then they told José not to let him back into the house. The creep is six feet two, and José is five three - when he stands up straight – and weighs about a hundred and ten.'

'He messed you up,' Jill realized in sudden indignation. 'You've got a cut on your shoulder.'

Chris shrugged. 'It's just a scratch – he got worse.'

'You need an antiseptic,' she insisted. 'Sit down – I've got bacitracin and bandages in my medicine chest.'

Chris grimaced.

'You don't want to pick up an infection your first day on the job.' Chris was pleased that he had managed to land a job in publishing.

'Okay, Florence Nightingale, do your thing.'

All at once Jill realized she was wearing only her short nightie. And the glint in Chris's eyes said he found the view most interesting.

Jill lay in bed – knowing she wouldn't fall asleep again. That poor little kid. No more than two. Chris said he was standing up in his crib – crying his little heart out. That was so sweet of Chris to run up that way. He could have been badly hurt.

Was she misinterpreting that glint in his eyes, while she was fixing the cut on his shoulders? *Is he gay?*

Despite her conviction that she wouldn't go back to sleep, she dozed at brief intervals. At moments past seven she abandoned bed to shower, prepare for the business day. She left her bedroom, headed for the kitchen. She'd grab a glass of juice, pick up breakfast en route to the office.

She was aware of the aroma of brewing coffee. Chris emerged from the kitchen with a dazzling smile.

'Coffee will be ready in a minute,' he reported. 'Sit and be served. Oh, how do you like your eggs?' He chuckled. 'And they are your eggs – I'll shop on the way home from the office.'

'If I don't have to make them, I'll take them any way.' She laughed at his reproachful expression. 'Scrambled preferred.'

She sat in their dining area at the bistro table – bought because of its low price-tag – and waited to be served.

'How do you like your coffee?' he called from their galley kitchen.

'Hot, black, and sweet,' she called back. *I could get used to this.*

Chris brought her a mug of coffee. The oversized mug she favored. He was singing – slightly off-key – an old Peter, Paul & Mary favorite, written before he was born. So he liked folk music. Okay, that was good. She wouldn't have to worry about his playing hard rock on the stereo Sandy had left behind in her bedroom.

'I gather you expect to like your job,' she commented while he brought plates of scrambled eggs and toast to the table. 'You're headed for work in a good mood.'

'I'll die of boredom within a week – but I'll stay with it. I want to learn the business. A substantial promotion within six months,' he predicted. *He'll need it – to pay his share of the rent.* All at once he was somber. 'I hated my last job. When it folded, I swore to stay out of the field. My old man is pissed that I came down to New York to work in publishing. He wanted me to move into investment banking – he had this connection.' Chris grimaced.

Jill was startled. 'That's my field. My father was in it, too – until he skipped out and ran off to South America.' *Why am I talking this way to Chris?*

'I might as well be in South America. My father and I aren't on speaking terms. I failed him.' Chris gestured grandly. 'I

114

don't know how it happened. You know how these things esca-
late. We both said things we didn't mean – and I took off.'

'I have no desire to talk to my father.' All at once Jill was
bitter. 'I'll probably never see him again – and that's just fine
with me.'

'My mom's upset,' Chris said after a moment. 'But it's my
life.' Now he forced a more casual note. 'So, how do you like
investment banking?'

'I like the money.' She was honest. 'I hate the hours. I'm
not sure how long I'll stay with it. A friend of mine just opened
a publicity firm with her boyfriend. They're very excited
about it.'

'I'm excited about being in publishing – even at the bottom.
But I don't intend to stay there. I'm moving up. It's in the
cards—' His smile was brilliant.

'I'd better get moving to my office.' *Is he really gay?* 'I've
got a rough day ahead of me.'

'Finish your breakfast,' he ordered with mock sternness.
'Here I slaved over a hot stove,' he clowned.

'If you bring me another mug of coffee,' she stipulated.
*He's such a sweet, bright guy. But he must be gay. Theresa
wouldn't lie to me.*

*So what if he isn't gay? I have no room in my life for a
guy. Not even for a puppy. When would I have time to walk
him? Or her?*

Twenty-Four

This week was running past, Claudia thought as she walked
through the early morning quietness to her cubicle in
Michael's suite. Here it was, Friday already.

'Hi, you're running late,' Dolores teased at her approach. 'I beat you in by six minutes.' On most mornings Dolores trailed by ten or fifteen minutes.

'I'll have to do better.' Claudia's smile was warm. She would miss the camaraderie here, she thought wistfully. But, most of all, she'd miss Michael.

'Michael said to send you in as soon as you arrived,' Dolores reported. 'He already ordered me to have coffee sent up. It's on the way.'

'Is he in a rotten mood?' Claudia asked, hanging away her coat and thrusting her purse into its usual resting place.

'He's uptight.' Dolores shrugged good-humoredly. 'But when isn't he uptight?'

Michael was at his desk – scanning a group of proposed mailings.

'Hi. Sit,' he told her. 'I need to break down promotion for the months we haven't covered.'

'Okay.' She understood. He wanted her reactions as a prospective woman customer.

'We've covered the Christmas situation.' He rose to his feet and began to pace. 'We have to focus on the pre-Easter period, the pre-July 4th weekend and approaching summer, the opening of the school year.' He frowned, stared into space. 'What are we missing?'

'Thanksgiving.'

'I've ordered the main floor to arrange Thanksgiving decorations throughout that floor.' He stopped dead – almost like a prosecuting attorney, Claudia thought. 'What else can we do to bring in customers pre-Thanksgiving?'

She'd been thinking about this in a corner of her mind. 'What about distributing pamphlets – a Thanksgiving minicookbook? They could be handed out at the door—'

'Not at the door,' he rejected. 'We want to get these women onto the selling floor—' He squinted in thought, shook his head. 'So women are intrigued by this offer. We no longer have a kitchen department.'

In truth, like some other stores Miller's has become almost

116

*a huge specialty shop. Floor space is too expensive to be
allotted to a low-earning department.*

'But it'll bring women into the store.'

'Where do we distribute these mini-cookbooks?' Before she
could answer, he picked up his own new thought. 'At a table
set up near the bank of elevators.' At the rear of the selling
floor.

'We'll have to get permission to use recipes,' she reminded.
Will we have time to do that?

'No,' he rejected with an air of triumph. 'Between us we
have recipes—' He paused. His eyes held hers. All at once
this was an achingly personal moment. *He's remembering our
being together in his apartment.* And then the moment was
over. He was the Miller's troubleshooter – determined to turn
the store's bottom line around. 'You have original ones?'

'I make my own recipes,' she admitted. 'You know – health-
conscious decisions.' *He does know – he does the same. Oh,
we do think alike in so many ways. Though where I'm impulsive, he considers more carefully. Why does he insist he's not
a free man? That's all that's keeping us apart. He's divorced
– I'm divorced. Why can't we live for each day? Who's to be
hurt?*

'It'll be a mini-cookbook – with just Thanksgiving recipes,'
he pinpointed. 'Between us we can do it.' He exuded satisfaction. 'Now, what else can we do?'

'We might have a story hour for pre-schoolers,' she plotted.
'To teach them about the first Thanksgiving.'

'Tied in with discount coupons for that day,' he pounced.

'A double incentive for mothers with small children to come
into the store.' *He likes the idea.*

But now he appeared skeptical. 'Can you dig up an enter-
tainer to handle it at this late date?'

Her mind moved into high gear. 'I can.' Jill had talked about
a client of her friend Diane. A woman who offered storytelling
in conjunction with hand puppets. Jill said Diane was plan-
ning a promotion in anticipation of the woman's agent landing
a TV show for her. 'But I'll have to get on it fast.'

'Do it. And we need to work on the Thanksgiving mini-cookbook fast.' He seemed to be in some troubling inner debate. Claudia waited. 'Will you be busy tomorrow night?'

'No.' Her heart began to pound.

'Then let's work on the cookbook tomorrow at dinner. Talk to Dolores about alerting our printer that we'll need it in a hurry.'

Both started at the light knock on the door that said Dolores was about to join them.

'Claudia, there's a call for you.'

'Oh, I'm sorry—' She turned to Michael in apology.

'No reason to be. Go take your call.'

'Michael, you have to leave in a few minutes for your lunch date with the ad agency people,' Dolores reminded him.

Michael grunted. 'Damn, I'd forgot all about it. Thanks, Dolores.'

Claudia hurried to her cubicle, picked up her phone. *Nobody has this number except the kids and Shirley. What's up?* 'Hello.'

'Mom, I checked my email when I left for the office this morning,' Jill said. 'This is the first chance I had to call. I don't know how Dad's connections handled it so fast – but the divorce is final. The papers are in the mail.' Hostility crept into Jill's voice. 'He couldn't wait to tell you.'

'Telling me made him feel free,' Claudia said with a coolness that was fabricated. 'Is it legal here in this country?'

'There's some kind of agreement between the countries – it's legal,' Jill assured her. She hesitated. 'I checked it out with one of the firm's attorneys.'

'I'm glad it's over. Thanks for letting me know, darling.'

'I have to go to a meeting now. Brunch Sunday morning?'

'That'll be great.'

'At the Lyric. Same time,' Jill said with an air of haste. 'See you there.'

Claudia sat motionless – absorbing the brief conversation with Jill. Twenty-two years of her life had just been officially wiped off the slate. But she felt no sense of loss, she realized. Not for Todd's place in her life. It would take a while to cope with the financial loss – but she would survive. The kids would survive.

She glanced at her watch. Fran would be going out for lunch. Try to catch her before she left. They'd lunch together. Today she wouldn't settle for a sandwich at her desk.

She emerged from the elevator on Fran's floor. Fran was walking towards her with a welcoming smile.

'Hey, are you out of the salt mine for lunch?'

'I'm living dangerously,' Claudia flipped. 'Let's lunch on my expense account.' *Michael won't mind.* 'The Oasis.'

'Wow!' Fran grinned. 'You do have perks.'

As Claudia had anticipated, the Oasis was lightly populated. They settled themselves at a table that provided privacy. Fran kicked off her shoes. A waiter came to take their orders. They debated, made their choices.

'I've been working here almost eighteen years,' Fran reminded when their waiter departed, 'and even with my side business I can't afford to eat here.' A familiar glint in her eyes. *Fran still thinks there's something more than business between Michael and me. How I wish there was!*

'That's a long haul,' Claudia acknowledged.

'I'm going to my brother in Ridgefield for Thanksgiving,' Fran reported, and Claudia was suddenly tense. *It's so close! I've lost track of time. The kids and I will have Thanksgiving together. So it'll be in my tiny sublet – we'll be together. That's what counts.*

'This is my month to live it up.' Fran sighed. 'All this talk about low inflation. The insurance on my apartment just went up eleven percent. You don't get health insurance from the store—' Claudia nodded in agreement. 'The store just notified us that beginning in February of next year we're to pay twenty-five percent of the monthly premiums.'

'I don't have health insurance,' Claudia admitted with a fresh surge of alarm. 'Neither does Larry. Jill does, through the company.'

'That's living dangerously.' Fran was somber.

'That's me and how many millions of Americans?'

'Have you noticed how packaging in the supermarkets is dropping in size?' Fran grunted in distaste. 'What used to be sixteen ounces is now twelve or thirteen – but the price is the same. Do they think the public is too dumb to notice?'

'I've become a reader of the supermarket circulars – but everybody is doing the same,' Claudia said. 'All these women – and some men – walk through the aisles checking the "specials."'

'Oh, I have pictures of my brother and sister-in-law's kids.' Fran was digging into her purse. 'They're gorgeous and so smart.'

Claudia made the required comments, smiled as Fran extolled the virtues of her two nephews and her niece. But her mind was off in other areas.

Todd's no longer a part of my life. And Shirley's right – God willing, I have a lot of years ahead of me. Why must Michael's ex-wife stand between us?

I want him to be part of my life. He wants that, too. How do I make him understand we mustn't deprive ourselves of something so beautiful? He won't fight for us – but I will.

Twenty-Five

Saturday morning Claudia awoke with instant realization that this evening she would be working with Michael at his apartment. She was conscious of a surge of anticipation. She'd never felt this way about any man. Not even Todd in those early years.

Only now could she be honest with herself. She'd been alone and lost when Mom and Dad died in that plane crash. So vulnerable when Todd pursued her. And in those days Todd had been another man – with ideals she shared. But she'd never felt for Todd what she felt for Michael.

She heard the sound of rain pounding the windowpanes. Another dreary weekend. Yet there was a serenity about rainy days and nights that she liked – when life was on an even keel.

Why is Michael so insistent on avoiding a relationship with me? We have so much to give to each other. Who's to be hurt?

She thought about Michael's baby daughter – who'd lived only a few minutes. He would have been such a fine father. How awful, to have been caught in such a situation. An invalid wife who was draining him dry. And instantly she was ashamed of this feeling. Of course, a man like Michael wouldn't shirk his responsibilities. *But why deprive us of what will hurt nobody?*

It would take time, she acknowledged, for Larry to accept Michael in her life. Jill would be astonished but would approve. They'd still be her kids – she wouldn't love them less. But Michael would have none of it, she reminded herself again. How could she change his thinking? Because if she didn't – and her job fizzled out with the new year as seemed likely – she'd never see him again.

In a flood of frustration she tossed aside the comforter and headed for the bathroom to shower and prepare for the day. The realization that Thanksgiving was fast approaching was unnerving. The first Thanksgiving the kids had ever known without Todd.

Not that Todd had ever been a real participant, she taunted herself. He'd spend most of the day watching football or sports news. Larry and Jill would sleep late, come into the kitchen to make lively comments about dinner preparations.

At one point – in younger years – they'd fought about who'd make the cranberry sauce while she was tending to other chores. They'd argue good-humoredly about how she was to spice up the pumpkin pie – with rum or Bailey's Irish Cream. It was always a warm, loving day. Neither she nor the kids realized Todd wasn't truly a part of it. Or did they?

Under the hot, stinging spray she remembered Larry's phone call last night. Poor darling, he was so concerned about her. But she'd made it clear – yet again – that she'd be terribly upset if he quit school to look for a job

She was just out of the shower when the phone rang. She hurried to pick up. Why did she always tense when the phone rang early in the morning or late at night?

'Hello.'

'Claudia, I wanted to catch you before you left the house.' A buoyant quality in Shirley's voice. 'I made Bill go for another echocardiogram – the way you insisted. His doctor called a few minutes ago – he's at the hospital making his morning rounds. He didn't come right out and say somebody messed up – I don't know if the cardiologist who read the test for him made a mistake or he read the wrong test – but Bill's okay. No heart problems.'

'Shirl, that's wonderful!' Claudia took a deep breath of relief.

'He just kept telling Bill, "You're okay, you're a healthy man." Bill didn't push for any further clarification. God, I was scared—'

'I know.' At intervals in the past five days she'd asked herself if Bill had gone for the second echocardiogram. She should have called, she reproached herself now. But Shirl knew how crazy her life was these days. 'Do something special tonight – to celebrate.'

'I'm calling the babysitter. Bill's taking me out to an unbelievably expensive restaurant for dinner. Thank God for credit cards!'

As usual on Saturdays Claudia arrived at the office two hours before Dolores surfaced. She knew Michael was in his office, though he didn't emerge until almost noon. He was oddly somber.

'You're okay for this evening?' he asked.

'Sure.' Her smile was tentative. *Is he about to cancel?*

'I've been working you like a dog.' He was contrite. 'Let's

play truant, cut out around four o'clock.' Unexpectedly he grinned. 'There's skating on TV from four thirty to six p.m. My two passions,' he reminded, 'are figure skating and cooking.' *He's telling me again that there's no room in his life for me.* 'I gather you share these.'

She managed a warm smile. 'Oh, yes.' *And more.*

'All right. We get out of here at four o'clock.' His answering smile was a dismissal.

At a few minutes before 4 o'clock Michael called Claudia into his office, closed the door.

'Lest we start weird rumors,' he began self-consciously, 'I'll leave in a couple of minutes. You follow a few minutes later. I'll be waiting at the northwest corner – we'll pick up a cab there.'

'Good thought.' She was casual. *Are people talking about Michael and me?*

On schedule Michael left the office – exchanging good-humored barbs with Dolores about working half a day. A few minutes later Claudia reached for her coat, pulled it on.

'Another deserter?' Dolores drawled, eyebrows lifted.

'I have to meet Jill,' she fabricated. 'We're going to shop a birthday present for Shirley.' She'd talked to Dolores about Shirley when they were discussing best friends.

'Why not buy it here and get your employee discount?'

'There's a fancy cooking gadget Shirl mentioned.' Miller's had dropped their kitchen department three years earlier. 'Jill says we'll find it in Macy's.'

Dolores winced. 'Okay – be a traitor. Go shop in Macy's.'

Claudia hurried from the office, out of the store and to the corner where Michael said he'd be waiting. It wasn't a date – but it wasn't business, either, to be watching figure skating together. Should she have offered to bring dessert? she asked herself belatedly.

Shoulders hunched against the blustery wind that had come up during the day, she sought for Michael – for an instant fearful that he wasn't there.

123

'Hi.' He moved into view.

'Hi.' *This feels like a date. But how would I know? I haven't dated in twenty-two years.*

'It's blowing up a storm again.' His hand shot up as a cab slid into view.

The cab pulled to a stop. They moved inside. Michael gave the driver his address and leaned back, stifling a yawn.

'I was up till almost two this morning – trying to remember recipes, scribbling down notes.' He patted his briefcase. 'I'm sure you've come up with a few?' His eyes were inquiring.

'I made some notes last night,' she admitted. 'I don't suppose we have to try them all out? I mean,' she said awkwardly because the way he was gazing at her was unnerving, 'our kitchens have been our labs in the past.'

'The skating will be our reward before we settle down to business.' Now he was brisk. 'Dolores said she'd talked with our printer. He wants finished copy in his hands by Wednesday morning.'

'That shouldn't be a problem.' She remembered – how many years ago was it? – when she'd been part of a volunteer group that brought out a cookbook compiled by members. That had taken many months. 'It's a pamphlet – not a whole cookbook.'

'The more I think about it, the more I like the idea. And if it goes over here, I'll suggest it be used next year for the whole chain.'

All at once he was silent, staring into space. His face grim. 'I'm not sure where I'll be next year—'

'Oh?' Claudia was unnerved.

'That internal battle going on in Chicago. Either I'll be out on my butt – or, my mole tells me, after New Year's I'll be shipped out to the next trouble spot. Los Angeles.'

Twenty-Six

By the time the cab driver pulled up before Michael's apartment building, the rain was coming down in torrents. Michael paid the driver, reached to open the door.

'Let's make a run for it.'

They dashed into the building while thunder rumbled overhead.

'It's really coming down,' the doorman greeted them. His eyes rested approvingly on Claudia.

It's rare for Michael to bring anyone home with him. He surmises we're having an affair. Does he remember I've been here before?

Michael glanced at his watch as they approached the elevators. 'We're in time for the opening,' he said with satisfaction. 'I don't know who's skating – but if it's Yagudin and Plushenko, I'll be in heaven.'

'And Elena and Anton,' Claudia added. No need for second names – Michael would know. 'The Russians are wonderful – poetry on ice.'

Michael's first move on walking into the apartment was to rush to turn on the television set. The prior program was just ending.

'Let me have your coat. I'll hang it in the bathroom to dry.'

'The program's starting,' Claudia called after him and sat on the corner of the sofa.

Michael returned to the living room, hesitated a moment, sat in the club chair. *He doesn't trust himself to sit next to me.*

The skating was superb. Ostensibly, both Claudia and Michael were aware of nothing else. Yet she was conscious of the way Michael rushed into casual conversation about the skaters on each commercial break – as though to deny his inner emotions.

At the final commercial break, Michael headed for the kitchen to check on the crockpot.

'The timing is perfect. I just have to add a tiny bit of cream.' He chuckled at her raised eyebrows. 'Actually it's half-and-half – and just a couple of tablespoons for the whole crockpot.'

'That's acceptable,' she approved.

'Dinner will be simple – give us time to settle down to work,' he said self-consciously, returning to the living room. *He's telling me that's why I'm here. To work.* But his eyes made a different statement. 'The crockpot rules again.'

They made a game of setting the table, preparing a salad to accompany the crockpot main course – a chicken, white wine, and mushroom masterpiece. Claudia put up coffee – after piercing the atmosphere with the screech of the coffee grinder.

At the table Michael immediately launched into a dissertation about Thanksgiving recipes. 'I remember the Thanksgivings when I was at home with my parents.' His voice tender. 'The three of us involved in getting dinner on the table.' He took a deep breath. 'That's long gone.'

'I always loved Thanksgiving. In my growing-up years, the years when the kids were growing up.' Where would Michael spend Thanksgiving? Alone here in the apartment? In a corner of her mind she remembered Shirley's suggestion that she invite Michael to have Thanksgiving dinner with her and the kids.

No, I can't do that. The kids wouldn't like it. He'd probably refuse. I'd scare him to death. An aggressive woman. His ex-wife was like that, wasn't she?

'I remember my last Thanksgiving with my parents – when I came back from the Peace Corps.' His face was suffused with tenderness. 'They were such good people. Lisa – my ex-wife – insisted on going out to a fancy restaurant for every major holiday. Now she's a bitter, angry woman – pushing the days away in her Arizona condo, with a live-in practical nurse to care for her. Not the life she'd expected.' *An expensive lifestyle that kept Michael hostage.*

Now Michael focused on the chicken. 'Perhaps I should have added more white wine to the crockpot—'

'No, it's perfect.' She dug into the chicken with gusto.

'I suppose it would be traitorous to include recipes for something other than turkey,' he said after a moment of thought.

'No,' she rejected. 'We could list them as a substitute for people who're allergic to poultry. I suppose that happens—' *He's not thinking about recipes – not when he looks at me like that.*

'I was uptight last night – about that rumor from Chicago,' he added. 'When I'm uptight, I bake. I made my version of chocolate tiramisu.'

'Oh, great. One of my all-time favorites.' *He's so torn – so sure he can't allow himself another life.* 'Even though I shudder at the ingredients that go into it.'

'Oh, I take detours.' His eyes lit with laughter. 'I replace the mascarpone with low-fat cream cheese, low-fat chocolate pudding – and go very light on the whipped cream. It's being only slightly wicked.'

They lingered briefly over dessert and coffee. It was clear that Michael was anxious to get down to the work at hand. *Because that's safe.*

'I'll throw the dishes into the dishwasher.' Michael pushed back his chair. 'We'll clear the table and work here. You brought recipes—' It was a statement rather than a question.

'They're in my purse. Typed in the rough. We'll make any changes you see fit.'

With the table cleared they settled themselves at it to focus on recipes. For an unwary – unintentional – instant their knees touched under the table. The atmosphere suddenly tense.

'Sorry.' He made an effort at amusement. 'I'm not making a pass.'

I wish he would. It's torture, sitting here with him this way and knowing he wants to make love as much as I do. He's so warm and tender and compassionate. And so bright. Why can't he see what we could share?

They went over recipes one by one, discarding some –

holding others. Each making contributions. The hours racing past.

'We'd better stop adding to the "use" pile,' Michael said wryly. 'Remember, we're compiling a mini-cookbook – not a full-scale cookbook.'

'Right.' *But I don't want to stop because that means I'll be leaving Michael.*

'You've been wonderful about all this,' he said.

'It's been fun.' She was conscious of a tightness in her throat.

'I wish we'd met at another time—' A sense of loss in his voice.

'Sometimes people have to live for the moment—' Her eyes held his.

'You'd only be hurt—' No pretense now. Hunger in his own eyes.

'Not if we live one day at a time,' she whispered. 'No commitments on either side—'

'Oh God, Claudia, I wish I could accept that—' His hand reached out to cover hers.

'I won't be hurt. Nobody will be hurt—'

'It's been such torment, being with you every day – telling myself there could be nothing for us.'

'There can be,' she said with a brilliant smile, realizing his capitulation. Rising to her feet. Impatient to be in his arms.

'I have such obligations—' But he was on his feet, reaching to draw her close.

'Each day we're together will be a precious gift,' she promised, while his mouth reached for hers and his hands fondled with hunger.

She felt born again. Savoring first love. *This is right. So right.*

She lay in the curve of Michael's arm. Fully awake. Exhilarated. A light comforter wrapped about them. Michael was asleep, his arms holding her prisoner – as though fearful she might walk out of his life.

Her eyes sought for her watch. It was past 2 a.m.! She must get home. Not that Jill or Larry would be apt to call on a Saturday night. For the young it was partying night. She felt a flicker of pleasure. Tonight she and Michael were young.

Careful not to awaken Michael, she moved his arm, left the bed. Her clothes lay in an abandoned heap on the floor. She dressed swiftly, slid her feet into her shoes.

'Claudia—' His voice was a caress. 'Don't go.'

'I must,' she apologized, and laughed at this decision. 'I know – it's ridiculous to expect a call from Jill or Larry on a Saturday night. But I wouldn't want them to call and find I wasn't home. They'd be alarmed.'

'I'll take you home.' He rose to his feet, began to dress.

'Michael, you don't need to do that. I'll grab a cab.'

'You're not going home alone at this hour of the night.' He was insistent. 'Claudia, I love you—' But his eyes were somber. It was as though he was saying, 'This is a love I can't afford.'

'I love you,' she whispered. For an instant she thought he would abandon dressing, reach for her again.

'Tonight was a magnificent gift.' *He makes it sound an aberration.*

'There can be more—' It was a blend of defiance and plea.

'I've never felt this way about anyone.' But already she felt unease infiltrating him. *Is he afraid he'll be diverted from earning the kind of money he needs to care for his ex-wife? Or is he worried his obligations will grow? I won't let myself be a financial burden.*

'Michael, nobody will be hurt,' she vowed. 'We'll take each day at a time. No commitments.'

Each day would be a precious gift. Yet she feared the ambivalence she sensed in him.

Twenty-Seven

Claudia and Michael left his apartment, hand in hand walked out into the night. The rain was over. A sliver of moon crept from behind a cloud. Here and there a cluster of people in a Saturday night mood punctured the 2 a.m. quiet.

A cab approached. Michael lifted an arm. The driver pulled up at the curb. With the traffic late-night light, the cab arrived at Claudia's building in minutes.

'Wait, please,' Michael instructed the driver, 'I'll be right back.'

He walked with Claudia into her lobby, past the doorman to the bank of elevators. He brought her hand to his mouth. His eyes inquiring yet wistful. 'You're probably busy tomorrow—' More statement than question.

'I'm meeting Jill for brunch,' she told him, 'and then I have to do all the weekend things – like laundry and apartment cleaning.'

His smile was wry. 'The universal occupation. See you Monday.' He hesitated an instant, leaned forward for a light kiss, and left with sudden speed. *Before he invited himself up? He would have been welcomed.*

Inside her apartment she automatically turned to her answering machine. The little red light was flickering. Jill had a conflict tomorrow morning, she guessed, and hurried to punch the 'play' button.

'Saturday, one-oh-two a.m.,' the recorded voice intoned. Claudia stiffened in alarm. Larry's voice – tense, almost frightened – drifted into the room.

'Mom, I'm all right – don't worry about me. I left work early because of this damn cold. I was mugged by a couple of creeps just outside the bar. I'm in the hospital Emergency now. I have only a hairline fracture in my left arm, but they're keeping me here overnight. Just for observation. I gave them my Health Insurance card. Are we still insured or did the insurance lapse when Dad walked out? Anyhow, don't worry – I'm okay. I'll call you in the morning.'

Her heart was pounding. What an awful experience for him! *Why are they keeping him overnight? What isn't he telling me?*

Could their insurance still be in effect? She'd assumed it wasn't – but she wasn't thinking clearly. As a college student under twenty-two he'd been covered by the family policy. Was there a chance that it wouldn't lapse until the end of the quarter? Todd walked out in late October – the last quarter of the year.

She'd call Jill. Maybe Jill knew about these things. Not now, she rejected. With Jill's crazy schedule she tried to catch up on sleep over the weekends. Talk to Jill at brunch. By then she should have heard from Larry.

Michael said she'd receive a bonus for her non-selling services. Would it be enough to handle Larry's hospital bill if there was no insurance coverage? Considering this, she winced. Even an overnight stay could run into thousands of dollars.

Would the hospital check on his insurance policy before they released him? She was conscious of a tightening in her throat. *This is what forty-three million Americans without health insurance face every day.*

Larry didn't say what hospital he was in – she couldn't try to call him. He'd said he'd call in the morning. She'd have to wait to hear from him again. He was nineteen years old – he shouldn't have to be terrified about a hospital bill.

If I have to pay it, we'll have a big hole in his tuition money for next semester. Damn Todd for putting us in this situation.

She forced herself to prepare for bed. Knowing sleep would be elusive. Had Larry suffered just a 'hairline fracture' in his arm or was there more? He was so protective of her.

He'd called after 1 a.m. – and she wasn't here. Had he been alarmed? She should have been home – where he expected her to be.

The first streaks of dawn were creeping through a chink in her bedroom drapes when she drifted into troubled slumber.

She awoke with a start five hours later. The phone was ringing. She rushed to pick up.

'Hello.'

'Mom, I'm at the apartment. I checked out with no sweat. The hospital didn't say anything about our policy being cancelled. I guess it's okay. Dad's policy must have operated on the quarter system – we're covered until the end of the year.'

'Darling, what a terrible experience. How do you feel? What did the doctors say?' Her mind was flooded with questions now.

'Like I told you, it's just a hairline fracture. They gave me painkillers in case I need them. It's my left arm – I can manage most things. I'll have to miss work for a few days,' he conceded.

'I'll send you a check,' Claudia said quickly.

'Mom, you don't have to do that—' But he didn't sound convincing.

'I can manage,' she insisted. She'd be paying the apartment rent in a lump sum – when Laura returned from Iraq. She'd have her bonus money by then. 'Will two hundred be enough to see you through?'

'Sure, Mom, but I don't think you should—'

'I'm getting a bonus because of this side assignment,' she interrupted. Michael never hinted at how much it would be – and she wouldn't receive it till the end of the year, she gathered. 'I'll mail the check first thing in the morning. Priority mail. But you won't get it until Tuesday – the post office doesn't pick up on Sundays—'

'That'll be fine,' Larry soothed and paused. 'You're sure you can handle this?'

'I can manage, darling.' *My baby and he's worried about taking money from me.*

'Mom, you're the best—'

'I love you,' she said softly. 'You and Jill are my whole world.'

Off the phone she struggled for calm. So they had hospitalization – at least until the end of the year. Then what? She'd have to find a job that provided health insurance for its employees – or made a major contribution to this.

As a temporary employee at Miller's she wasn't entitled to health insurance. Was there a possibility that she'd be held on after the holidays? Not a chance if Michael was sent to Los Angeles, she taunted herself. *I don't want to think about Michael's being three thousand miles away.*

In a corner of her mind she remembered Fran's unhappiness that the store was stipulating employees were to pay 25% of their health insurance starting in February of next year. She'd be thrilled with that kind of a deal, since Fran said children under twenty-three and in school were covered by the store policy.

She'd never realized until now that health insurance was so important for working people. High even for single people – unnerving for families. *Jill is covered – but I have to provide for Larry. Maybe Michael is right. There's no room in either of our lives for the other.*

The Lyric was crowded when Claudia arrived – the atmosphere convivial. A line waited for seating. Her eyes searched the room – not expecting Jill to be there as yet. But there she was – in a rear booth. A hand raised in welcome. The smart office attire replaced today by jeans and blue turtleneck. Dark hair tied back in a ponytail.

Claudia moved past the line, hurried to Jill. 'You're early.' She slid into the seat opposite Jill, pulled off her jacket. 'Your clock running fast?' she joshed because Jill was known to arrive at most appointments at the very last moment.

'I got up earlier than normal.' Jill giggled. 'Chris persuaded me to jog with him in the park. He's a bigger health nut than you.'

'Talking about health,' Claudia said wryly, 'Larry landed in the hospital Emergency last night—'

'Oh, my God! What happened? Is he okay?'

'He says he's fine. He has a hairline fracture in his left arm.' *I'll call him tonight, to reassure myself. I wish I could drive out there and see for myself.*

Now she reported on Larry's unexpected experience.

133

'Poor baby, he was scared to death that his health insurance policy wouldn't be accepted. But he said there'd been no questions.'

'You and Larry must be covered until the end of the year,' Jill surmised. 'If the policy had lapsed, the hospital computer would have shown it.'

'I need a job that provides family health insurance,' Claudia said grimly. But after the first of the year she wouldn't even have this job. *Will Michael be sent to Los Angeles? I know he doesn't want to go – but he can't give up a high-paying job.*

I was wondering—' All at once Jill seemed self-conscious. 'Will you want to bother with making Thanksgiving dinner – or should the three of us go out? My treat,' she added quickly.

Claudia winced. They'd never gone out to a restaurant for Thanksgiving dinner. It was a very special time – when loved ones should be together. At home. 'No way.' She rejected this. 'We'll have dinner at my apartment.' *Where the mother lives is home.*

'We'll have a turkey and all the trimmings,' Jill decreed.

She's remembering last Thanksgiving. When Todd was halfway across the country, said he'd settle for room service at his hotel. With that woman he must have married by now.

'I'll come over early and help.'

'Larry will be staying with me over the long weekend,' Claudia reminded. 'We'll have dinner mid-afternoon, as always.' Todd wouldn't be missed. He'd never truly shared the spirit of the day with the rest of the family. It was just a day to kick off his shoes and watch football on TV. Or make a business excuse to be away from the family – like on last Thanksgiving. Probably shared in some family restaurant with his South American slut.

'Would you be upset if I invited Chris for Thanksgiving dinner?' Jill asked. 'I mean, he's going to be all alone—'

'Of course I don't mind—' But her eyes were questioning. She felt a flicker of unease. Jill wasn't becoming emotionally involved with Chris, was she? She knew he was gay.

'It's just that I feel so sorry for him,' Jill explained. 'His father blew up when he turned down a job the old boy was arranging for him. They're not speaking. He'll be alone in the apartment on Thanksgiving.'

Claudia remembered the homeless kittens Jill had brought home through the years. *'Mom, they need a home.'* Was Chris another 'homeless kitten' – or more?

'Invite him,' Claudia ordered tenderly. Then a sudden thought sent her heart pounding. *Do I dare invite Michael? Yes!* 'I may invite my boss, too.' It was a casual statement. 'He's kind of a loner. He'd probably be eating dinner alone at a restaurant—'

'Single?' All at once Jill was interested.

'Divorced. No family, I gather.' *Jill doesn't suspect anything – she's just romanticizing.* 'I'm not sure he'll come—'

'Ask him.' Jill's smile was brilliant.

'I'll think about it,' Claudia hedged. 'Though it does seem the nice thing to do.'

Why does Jill keep looking at me that way? She can't know about Michael and me. But I'll ask him for Thanksgiving dinner. We'll play it cool – the kids will never guess how we feel about each other. Jill will decide it was just in her mind.

It can go nowhere. We both realize that. His ex-wife stands in the way. One day at a time – that's all we can expect.

Twenty-Eight

En route to the bus stop Jill spied an unoccupied cab. She lifted an arm in the familiar signal. Bad habit, she admonished herself. But she'd grown accustomed to cabs or car service since she started at the company. Time was at a premium on this job.

Settling into the cab, she thought about her mother. Mom had this low-paying job till the first of the year. Where would she go then? There was this awful age barrier that few talked about but everybody knew existed. Employers in Spain were more honest. She remembered the article she'd read in the *Times* or *Newsweek*. Classified ads were blunt: 'Only applicants attractive and under 35 need apply.'

As long as she had an apartment-sharer, she'd be able to help some. But that wouldn't go far. Maybe Mom and Larry should be realistic. He could transfer to a city college with tiny tuition and share Mom's apartment – as long as she had it. That was another bitchy problem. What happened when Mom got kicked out of the apartment?

Was she fantasizing or was there something between Mom and her boss? There was that look in her eyes when she talked about him. It was obvious he had a great job – and he was divorced. And she was inviting him to Thanksgiving dinner. How many employees would invite their boss to Thanksgiving dinner?

She was fighting off yawns as she approached her apartment door. She'd been out of her mind to allow Chris to drag her out to jog on a Sunday morning. Sunday mornings were for sleeping. But he had that warm, ingratiating way about him.

Key in hand, she paused. She could hear the vacuum cleaner running. She unlocked the door, walked inside, laughed at the sight of Chris straining to propel the vacuum cleaner behind the 32-inch television set.

'Chris, I have a cleaning woman coming in every Wednesday—'

He glanced up, grinned, flipped off the vacuum cleaner. 'Yeah, but she never goes behind things. She probably tells herself, "Hey, nobody looks back there."'

'I don't,' Jill acknowledged.

'It's a good workout. Cheaper than a gym.' But he appeared

ready to abandon the vacuuming. 'I've got coffee up – if you're interested.'

'I smell it.' She sniffed. 'I'm interested.' Thanksgiving was a week from the coming Thursday – it was time to invite Chris for dinner.

'Sit,' he ordered while he unplugged the vacuum cleaner, wrapped the cord about its resting place. 'Coffee coming up.'

'How's the job?' Jill asked, sliding out of her jacket and settling at the bistro table that comprised their dining-room furniture.

'Well, I haven't been voted in as CEO as yet,' he flipped. 'But I'm working on it. How's your job?' He poured coffee into the pair of oversized mugs that was his one contribution to the household.

'I'm working my butt off, but the money's great,' she admitted.

'You want out,' he decided.

'I can't afford out,' she tossed back. 'Not at the cost of living in the middle of Manhattan.' She brushed aside the mental observation that Larry might be needing financial assistance to stay in school – and where would Mom go when her sublet ran out?

'What would you really like to do with your life?' He brought coffee to the table, sat in the other bistro chair.

'I don't know—' She stared into space for a moment. 'Maybe move into public relations. Diane – this friend of mine from college – just opened her own firm with her boyfriend. They're both working like crazy – but they seem to be having fun. Everything seems a challenge.'

'I knew when I was twelve I wanted to do something in publishing.' He grinned. 'At one time I thought maybe I'd be the next Steinbeck – but gave that up fast. No talent. But I could still be part of the book world.' His face tightened. 'My old man is sure he knows everything about every business on the face of the earth. He said to work in publishing I'd need a trust fund – and that wasn't about to happen.'

'You won't be going home for Thanksgiving?'

'Are you kidding? I'm not even invited.' He shook his head in disbelief. 'I can't believe what's happened. My mom calls once in a while – but she doesn't want me to call home. She doesn't want him to know she talks to me. He'd consider that disloyal.'

'What about having Thanksgiving with us?' Jill asked casually. 'There'll just be Mom and Larry and me plus a friend of Mom's she's going to invite.'

He appeared startled, then almost disbelieving. 'You're inviting me for Thanksgiving dinner?'

'That's just what I said. You want a written invitation?'

His smile was dazzling. 'I'll accept a verbal one. Sure, I'll love to go to your Thanksgiving dinner. I'll bring a bottle of wine,' he added.

'You don't have to do that.' She knew his tight financial status.

'I want to do it.' Now he was somber. 'You know, this will be the first Thanksgiving in my life that I wasn't with the family. My sister and her husband will be flying in from Cleveland.'

Why doesn't his mother do something to mend fences with his father? Because his father is too stubborn to admit he made a mistake? No way would Chris make the first move. He's stubborn, too.

He's right – families should be together at Thanksgiving. But Dad is in South America and married to his bimbo. We'll probably never see him again. Why do I care? He was never much of a father

Walking to the office on this crisp, bright Monday morning, Claudia was conscious of the many empty storefronts along the way. Not only mom-and-pop shops, she realized. Major chains were closing stores that weren't earning their keep. Michael said it was the insane rents that were closing them.

Every time she turned on the TV there was a report of another pair of corporations merging and laying off workers.

Are we going to become a world of only huge conglomerates? That was scary.

Claudia walked with the lights, impatient to be at the store. Now she went over in her mind the work that lay ahead for the day. Michael said she was to focus on preparing the recipes for their Thanksgiving mini-cookbook. That was the prime objective for the next forty-eight hours.

'Add those flip comments we made when we were discussing each one. That's a good personal touch.'

He trusted her with this, she thought with pleasure. The store's full-page ad in the Sunday *Times* would feature the free mini-cookbook for all comers. The printer was standing by for copy. Please God, let it be a success. But in a corner of her mind she realized that Michael's success would add to the possibility of his being shipped out to Los Angeles – and she didn't want to think about that. She didn't want to think beyond the next five weeks.

Walking into the store, she saw several of the display people involved in setting up elaborate Christmas decorations. Thanksgiving hadn't arrived yet! She didn't want to think about Christmas. A few days after Christmas she'd be out of work – unless Michael remained at Miller's Manhattan and kept her on as his 'assistant.' *He doesn't want to go to Los Angeles. He knows if he does we'll never see each other again.*

'Look, we've got to be out of here in another hour,' one of the display crew exhorted the others. 'Move it!'

Claudia hurried through the store to the bank of elevators, as though to escape the reminder that time was running past. It was easy to say, 'Let's live one day at a time.' Harder to do.

Will I be making a mistake to invite Michael to Thanksgiving dinner? Will he back away, seeing me as a woman in pursuit? But I want Michael in my life. We've found something so beautiful. Let's hold on as long as we can.

Riding up in the elevator, she thought about Larry. Poor baby, what an awful experience! Perhaps she should have wired him money instead of sending a check. But he'd insisted it would be okay. And shouldn't they already be checking on schools – and financial aid for next year's schooling? Talk with Larry about it, she exhorted herself.

Every time her eyes fell on the calendar, she was conscious that time was running out on the apartment. She shivered, remembering the insane apartment rentals – not just in Manhattan, even in the other boroughs.

Michael was in his office already – as she'd expected. Walking into their suite, she could hear him on the phone – arguing with someone. They weren't the only ones whose business day started well before the conventional 9 a.m. So much for technology providing much leisure time.

Dolores wasn't at her desk. Right. Dolores had said she couldn't be in until 10 o'clock. She was going to an early morning dental appointment.

'This guy is great – but he's as slow as the store is in giving raises.'

Michael said Dolores remained in the job only because of the bad employment market. She wasn't sure of that. Dolores was devoted to Michael – in a maternal way. She gathered there'd been much moaning at the bar when he left the White Plains store. Only here was he encountering waves of hostility – because he was making changes and people preferred remaining in the old grooves.

She settled herself at her computer, thrust everything from her mind except the work at hand. She was startled – four hours later – at the sound of Michael's voice.

'Let's take a lunch break,' he called from the doorway of his office. 'I'll send downstairs for sandwiches. Turkey and decaf?'

'Great—' *Should I invite him for Thanksgiving dinner? Will he back away, feeling implications he's not ready to assume?*

Twenty minutes later Claudia heard Dolores talking with, she gathered, a waiter from the Oasis. Two minutes later Michael summoned her.

'Claudia, lunch.'

While they ate, Michael reported on some preliminary responses from the Chicago office on their experimental catalogue.

'So you see,' he summed up, 'we're not doing badly.'

'That's hopeful.' But Claudia was conscious that part of his mind was disengaged from business talk.

He poured more coffee for each of them, hesitated a moment, then crossed to close the door. He turned to her. His face exuded an inner, painful debate.

'I want to believe so much in what you said. About us – and taking each day at a time—' His eyes clung to hers.

'Each day will be a gift,' she whispered. 'Why deny ourselves?'

'Saturday night?' he asked after a moment. 'We'll go out for dinner – somewhere very special.'

'Let's have dinner at your apartment,' she said. 'It's fun to cook together.' But the luminous glow in her eyes said she anticipated much more.

'Why couldn't we have met a dozen years ago?' he asked yet again.

'Let's cherish what we can have—' *If we were in his apartment – not here in the office, where Dolores might walk in any minute – we'd make love. And it would be so sweet.* Now she abandoned doubts about the Thanksgiving dinner invitation. 'What are you doing for Thanksgiving?'

'Nothing.' He seemed startled. 'I'll spend the day at home. Thanksgiving dinner alone in a restaurant is depressing—'

'Jill is inviting a friend for dinner. A man—' She tried for a light note. 'So why shouldn't I invite someone, too? Would you like to join us for Thanksgiving dinner?'

For an instant she took his silence for rejection. Then he answered. His voice elated. 'That would be wonderful. For years I've dreaded every major holiday that came along. Even when I was with Lisa,' he admitted. 'She always insisted on going out to some overly expensive restaurant.' He managed a ruefully reminiscent chuckle. 'She never once threw a turkey into the oven—'

'Come over early Thanksgiving Day,' she ordered, 'and we'll throw the turkey into the oven together.'

'You'll make a pumpkin pie,' he guessed. 'From scratch.'

'Right. Laced with rum. That's to persuade Jill to try it. She's never truly liked pumpkin. I usually pick up something utterly decadent at a bakery for her.'

'We'll have two pies,' he decreed. 'I'll bring the second.'

Her face lighted. This was the right mood. 'What kind?'

'Grasshopper pie,' he decided with air of triumph. 'With plenty of crème de menthe and crème de cacao. But I promise nobody will get drunk.'

'Jill will love it – we all will,' she predicted.

'Thank you for sharing Thanksgiving with me. It'll be a very special day.'

The shrill ring of the phone was a jarring intrusion. His private line, kept open for calls from the Chicago office.

'Hello.' His voice was unintentionally terse, Claudia realized.

He listened now. Frowned. 'When would you like me to make the flight?' All at once he was tense. 'Yes, we'll work out the time. We'll discuss it after the Thanksgiving weekend.' He put down the phone, took a long, labored breath. 'That was Chicago. I'm to fly out to Scottsdale around the first of the year. They're considering opening a store there. Los Angeles will close after the first of the year.'

Claudia's heart was pounding. 'Does that mean you'll be transferred to Scottsdale?'

'It could do,' he acknowledged. 'Of all the towns in the world, why Scottsdale?' he agonized.

'Oh!' All at once Claudia understood. His ex-wife lived in Scottsdale.

'If I'm lucky,' he struggled to appear optimistic, 'it'll just be a matter of my looking over the area, checking on a location for the store. It can't be a major store, considering the size of Scottsdale. But it's a very monied community – it could be a sharp move.'

'Let's don't think about it until after the holidays,' she ordered. 'Like we said, "One day at a time."'

But the prospect of Michael's moving out of her life was devastating.

Thirty

Claudia suspected the new week would fly past. Michael was being flooded with questions from the Chicago office about his various proposals. He was searching for new angles.

Should they introduce music on additional floors? Should they set up additional ladies' lounges? Should they set up a special desk on the men's floor, where women shoppers could request advice?

On Tuesday and Wednesday evenings she and Michael had dinner on a tray in his office, remained at the store until past 9 p.m.

'You're my guinea pig,' he joshed as they prepared to break for the day on Wednesday. 'If you crinkle your nose in that reproachful way, I know I'm off-track.' But his eyes reflected anxiety.

'What do you hear from Chicago?' He'd had two long calls earlier, she recalled. Until now she'd hesitated to probe.

He took a deep breath, blew out slowly. 'My mole told me there've been heated discussions – pro and con – about adopting our proposals. Two on the Board think we're out of our minds. I suppose it could go either way—'

'The proposals are solid,' Claudia protested.

'The store deserves another year.' Michael grimaced in frustration. 'I'm praying we get it. I don't want to see all our people on the unemployment lines.' *But every day the news reported new mergers, more outsourcing – and more people left without jobs.*

Taking a cab home – a perk of the job for late-evening departures – Claudia fretted over the nearsightedness of some of the Chicago big wheels. Only a couple were against the changes, she remembered defensively. Resentful of changes that they hadn't instituted.

It would be a plum for Michael if his proposals went through on a national scale, Claudia told herself. They'd earn him a big bonus. But she was still unnerved about the possibility of his being transferred to set up the store in Scottsdale.

At touching moments Michael mentioned his anticipation of spending Thanksgiving Day with her and the kids. He was so alone, she thought tenderly. A man who would have been such a fine father.

She spoke each evening with Larry. *'Mom, I'm okay – the arm's doing fine. I'll return to my job at the bar on Friday evening.'* She'd have brunch on Sunday again with Jill. Each time they talked – on the phone – she sensed Jill's rising disillusionment with her future in the business world.

'My generation was told that the world was ours. That the feminists had done it all for us, and we'd be fine. We thought we were in control of our destinies, but we aren't. We do the same work as men – but men are paid more. And how many of us make it to the top?'

Claudia was relieved that she and Larry had arrived at a tacit understanding that right after the first of the year he'd look into the question of financial aid for college. Despite the bad labor market he talked optimistically about landing a summer job. He'd need every dollar he could put aside for the last two years at school.

On Thursday Fran called upstairs to suggest Claudia meet her for a muffin and coffee after work.

'I'm off at six – can you make it?' Fran asked. 'Or will you be tied up in the slave market?'

'Meet you at the downstairs entrance at a few minutes past six,' Claudia promised. *Fran sounds harried. She needs to talk about something. About rumors she's picked up at the store?*

At exactly 6:02 Claudia emerged from the main floor elevator and charged towards the entrance. The selling floor was busy, she noted in a corner of her mind. The store open late tonight.

'Hi—' Fran called as she approached. 'It's cold out.'

'When Dolores came back from lunch she said the temperature had taken a deep drop.' Claudia hastily buttoned the smart black cashmere coat that had cost more than she earned now in three weeks.

'Somebody in your weird office takes normal lunch hours,' Fran approved as they hurried out into the early evening cold.

Claudia chuckled. 'Dolores is still part of the slave trade. She's out and back in thirty minutes.'

They made their way to the coffee shop that provided low-fat muffins and superb decaf. Still uncrowded at this hour. They settled themselves in a booth at the rear.

'I may be going off decaf,' Claudia reported while they waited to order. 'You know all the talk about how great tea – particularly green tea – is for your health.'

Fran shrugged. 'That's this week. But I saw an item on TV a few weeks ago where some research study showed that in ten out of twelve restaurants when you order decaf you're probably served regular coffee. But I need my caffeine fix a couple of times a day.'

Their waitress arrived. They ordered. Fran talked enthusiastically about shopping this evening for presents to take to her niece and nephews in Ridgefield on Thanksgiving Day. Claudia waited for her to reveal what was bothering her. When her air of enthusiasm evaporated, Claudia knew she was ready to talk.

'I hear Miller's stock took a deep drop on the market,' Fran began uneasily.

145

'Honey, the stock market is crazy these days – it's forever going up or down. Don't worry about it.' Neither she nor Fran owned stock, but she understood Fran's anxiety.

'Rumors are running around again about the store closing after the first of the year.' Fran was doleful. 'What do you think?'

'I don't think that'll happen. Michael's working like mad.' Fran's eyes searched hers. Hopeful now. 'I can't say anything definite, but Michael's fighting with the big boys to keep the store running another year. To see if his proposals turn things around.'

'I've been thinking what I could do if it happens. I'll get a tiny pension – about a couple hundred a month. Ain't that somethin',' Fran drawled, 'after over seventeen years in the trenches?' She took a deep breath. 'Anyhow, I was thinking about maybe opening up a catering service. Not a piddling deal like selling my cakes. A full-time operation. Maybe we could go into it together.'

'I don't know where I'll be after Christmas – but I'll have to look for something with a regular salary,' Claudia pointed out.

'If nothing comes along, think about it.' *Fran's grasping for a tow line.* 'You know a lot of people—'

Claudia shook her head. 'Not anymore.' Fran knew about her life with Todd – no real friends there. Her only friends were Shirley and Bill and the other three women of the 'Fantastic Five.'

'Isn't this the pits? In the richest country in the world, we're sitting here worrying where we'll be working in a few weeks. One of the women on my floor told me she'd been out of work for twenty-seven weeks before she got this job. She'd gone through all her savings, maxed out her credit cards, was days from applying for welfare. And January 1st she'll be back in the same rat race.'

'Fran, there's no sense in working yourself up into a nervous breakdown.' Claudia was somber. 'Just take one day at a time. You have a minor safety valve,' she pointed out. One not open to her. 'A chunk of weeks of unemployment insurance – plus your cake sales.'

'You worry, too,' Fran accused. 'You, me and how many millions of others?'

'Between now and Christmas let's not worry.' Claudia struggled to appear optimistic. 'Like I said, let's take one day at a time.' A new way of life.

Thirty-One

A t noon on Friday the printer – as promised – delivered the Thanksgiving mini-cookbook, piled now in a corner of Michael's office.

'They look great.' Michael radiated approval as he inspected a copy. 'They'll go on the main floor first thing Monday morning. The ad appears in Sunday's *Times*. It's a little thing,' he conceded, 'but I suspect it'll bring women into the store.'

Dolores appeared in the doorway. A copy of the Thanksgiving mini-cookbook in one hand. 'Can I take a dozen home with me?' she asked. 'To give to friends—'

'Sure thing.' Michael grinned.

'Maybe we could have a supply of cookies on the table,' Claudia said. 'Pumpkin cookies.'

'Like at some book signings I've been to,' Dolores pounced. 'Where there're cookies women go. It wouldn't be a high-cost deal,' she pursued. 'I could arrange with a local bakery to make them up – according to the recipe here.'

'Do it,' Michael ordered. 'But they must use our mini-cookbook recipe. Claudia's recipe,' he added, his eyes resting on her.

'Done,' Dolores promised and retreated, closing the door

behind her. A gleeful glint in her eyes. *She saw the way Michael looked at me just now.*

Michael leaned across his desk to reach for her hand. 'I'm counting the hours until tomorrow night.'

'Our little touch of heaven,' Claudia said softly.

'I never dreamt I could feel this way—'

'Our second chance—' She frowned as the phone punctured the moment.

'I'll take the phone off the hook at the apartment,' he promised, reaching to pick up. 'Nobody will intrude.'

Arriving at her apartment, Claudia saw the blinking red light on the answering machine. Why did she always tense up this way when there was a message? Larry insisted he was back to normal. She must stop these nightly calls to him. Jill was probably still at the office. Probably Shirley, she guessed.

She hit the message button. The caller was Shirley. She punched in Shirley's number.

'Hello.'

'Hi, I just got home,' she told Shirley.

'I hope you're getting mucho overtime,' Shirley flipped.

'It'll come in my bonus. I haven't been given a figure, but I suspect it'll be good.' *Michael will see to that.*

'Since you won't be coming out for Thanksgiving, what about arranging to take off Saturday and running out this weekend?'

Claudia hesitated. There had never been secrets between Shirley and her. 'I have – kind of a date with Michael for Saturday night.'

'Well, it's about time,' Shirley approved. 'The working dinners were more than that—' A hint of approval in her voice.

'Yes,' Claudia conceded. 'We're taking one day at a time. I told you what his ex-wife did to him in the divorce settlement. He's in a financial bind as long as she lives. He can't afford two households – and my job prospects are bleak.'

'That could change, honey—' Shirley hesitated. 'His ex-wife's health is bad, I gather.'

Claudia felt a surge of guilt. 'Shirl, we can't think that way—'

'Like you said,' Shirley purred. 'Take one day at a time.'

On Saturday morning Claudia arrived at the store with a sense of eager anticipation. She reveled in the knowledge that this evening would mark a change in her relationship with Michael. No excuse about work requiring her presence in his apartment. This evening belonged to them alone.

Dolores arrived as usual at a few minutes to ten, announced that she would be leaving at 2 p.m.

'I'm going to a birthday party for my sixteen-year-old goddaughter.' Her eyes were tender. 'I can't believe she's that old!'

'I know what you mean,' Claudia said softly. 'Sometimes I can't believe Larry is almost twenty and Jill almost twenty-two. The years go so fast.' It was frightening sometimes.

They knew so little about Dolores' private life, Claudia realized with a flicker of guilt. Dolores was devoted to Michael – but they knew little about her life away from the office.

Claudia was grateful to be busy. She'd feared the day would drag. But at moments before 6 p.m. Michael decreed work was over for the day. His eyes glowed with promise. No work in his apartment this evening. This was their time.

She knew that Michael hoped she would remain overnight, yet she couldn't bring herself to do that. Not tonight. Not until Larry and Jill understood that Michael had become part of her life. Maybe after the Thanksgiving weekend. Larry would be back at school. Jill, bless her, would applaud this new, precious development in her life.

They walked swiftly through the main floor of the store and to the exit. If the staff were curious about their relationship, Claudia told herself with a defiant smile, so be it.

'You're cold—' Michael reached for her hand as she hunched her shoulders against the sharp wind that had come up. 'But you won't be for long—' His eyes bright with promise.

'Do we have to shop for dinner?' she asked while he hailed a cab.

'I did that last night. Sure you wouldn't prefer to go out?'

'No way.'

They settled back in the cab, Michael's hand clinging to hers. It seemed so natural for his mouth to find hers in the winter darkness of the cab. For this evening all their cares would disappear. They would exist – for a few hours – in this special world they'd discovered for themselves.

Hand in hand they walked into the lobby of his apartment building. Claudia saw the glint of recognition in the doorman's eyes. He approved, she told herself in soaring pleasure. Doormen knew so much about the lives of tenants. Who lived alone and saw no one. Who arrived home with a variety of partners.

'Good evening, Carlos.' Michael's voice buoyant. 'Getting colder out there—'

'Yes, sir.' *But Carlos knows we don't care. We'll be warm and cozy inside Michael's apartment.*

They made a major production of preparing dinner. The stereo providing a Schubert symphony. At intervals Michael brought preparations to a stop to pull her into his arms.

'I can't believe we can be together this way,' he whispered, swaying with her. 'I can't believe you've come into my life.'

They sat down to a sumptuous dinner. Michael talked about his early ambitions to open a restaurant. Claudia listening with loving intensity. *He's never talked this way to anyone else. He's opening up his whole life to me. I want us to go on forever.*

'In time,' he admitted with a wry grin, 'I visualized a chain. Not in huge numbers. A small, special restaurant in perhaps a dozen major cities – catering to diners who enjoy a fine meal that meets the criteria for a healthful meal. But I knew it was just a dream.'

'We should cling to our dreams.' Claudia's face was luminous. 'That's what keeps life exciting.' *I dream of our spending the rest of our lives together. Tonight I can believe that.*

Michael chuckled. 'Lisa was shocked by my interest in

150

cooking. It wasn't macho – men didn't belong in the kitchen.'

'She's never heard that male chefs run the kitchens in the world's finest restaurants?' Under the dining table their knees touched. Claudia was conscious of a surge of anticipation, of a faint sound of mounting passion from Michael.

'Could we hold off coffee and dessert for a while?' he whispered. 'I want so desperately to make love to you.'

'I want that, too—' She took his extended hand, allowed him to draw her to her feet . . .

They lay entangled beneath the light comforter, her head on his shoulder. The world seeming a beautiful place. For now.

'I don't want to move from this spot,' he murmured. 'I wish we could stay this way forever.'

'Dessert and coffee can wait a while,' she decreed. 'I feel so smug, so pleased with life.' For now, her mind mocked – but don't think beyond now.

A soft, brief sound emerged from somewhere in the bedroom.

'My fax machine,' he said in reproach and reached to switch on the bedside lamp. 'Can't Chicago leave me alone on a Saturday evening?' But he was withdrawing to respond.

Claudia pulled herself up against the headboard while Michael strode towards the fax machine, located across the room in what he called his office-at-home corner. She watched while he pulled a page from the machine.

'Damn!' he uttered in disgust. 'I don't believe this!' But clearly he did.

'Problems?' Her heart began to pound. *He's being shipped away. Now? Before the first of the year?*

'It's from Lisa—' He gave a long, tormented sigh. 'She needs seven thousand dollars. Immediately. For some fancy diagnostic cardiac test her internist at the Mayo Clinic ordered.'

'Oh, Michael—' *Is there no end to what she's doing to him?*

'I should be able to get a personal bank loan—' His face grew taut with resignation. 'Somehow I'll manage to meet the payments.'

151

Thirty-Two

Jill came awake reluctantly – conscious of the luscious aroma of fresh coffee brewing in the kitchen. She squinted at the clock on her night table. Time to get up. She was meeting Mom for brunch in an hour. She winced, remembering that she'd dozed at the movie she'd seen last night with Caroline. But Caroline admitted she, too, had drifted off into the wild blue yonder.

'Damn it, Jill – the company drains us for anything else. We've sold out our social lives for the big bucks. And at the end of the two-year stretch, most of us will land out on our asses.'

Jill pulled herself up into a semi-sitting position, considered her lifestyle. It was accepted among the ambitious young that the 9 to 5 jobs led nowhere. Anybody determined to move up spent long hours in the slave pits. But away from the office she was too tired for anything but sleep. Not cool.

A tentative – light – knock on her bedroom door brought her back to the moment.

'Yeah?'

'In the mood for coffee?' Chris asked blithely. 'Hazelnut—'

'I'll be right out—' She tossed aside the comforter, searched for slippers bedside.

'Breakfast?' he tempted now.

'I'm having brunch with my mother,' she called back, 'but pour the coffee.'

She enjoyed these brief encounters with Chris at odd times. Weekend mornings. Coming home at 3 a.m. to find him poring over a manuscript he'd surreptitiously brought from the office.

He lent adventure to these occasions, she analyzed. *He's a fun person.*

Moments later – a short robe over her shorter nightie – she hurried to join Chris at the breakfast table. It was her lack of social life, she told herself, that made Chris so appealing. *He's gay – he's not interested in me.*

'Chicks aren't supposed to look so alluring before they go through the make-up mill,' he chided, bringing two oversized mugs of coffee to the table. A cheese omelet waiting to be demolished.

'Make-up is for business days.' She reached for her mug, sipped with pleasure. 'You're in the wrong business. You should be starting up competition for Starbucks – with this kind of coffee.'

'I like my business. Oh, not the donkey work I'm doing now,' he conceded. 'I'm aiming for a spot as editor. Sure, it'll take a while – but I'll get there.' His eyes were quizzical. 'You're still chomping at the bit in your cage?'

'A chunk of the time.' She stared into space. *My friends think I have it made – I'm on the way to big bucks. So why do I feel so rebellious?*

'How's your friend doing? The one in public relations?' He dug into his cheese omelet with enthusiasm.

'You mean Diane.' She frowned in thought. 'We're both too busy to do more than talk on the phone for a few minutes once in a while. But she loves what she's doing. Light on profits. She scrounges to meet her bills.' Jill's smile was wry. 'For that she had to go to an Ivy League school?'

'But she likes what she's doing,' he pinpointed with an air of triumph. 'You can put in fourteen-hour days – but if you love your work, you don't even notice.'

'I've got to get moving. My mother thinks promptness is second to godliness.'

'I'm still invited to Thanksgiving dinner?' An odd insecurity, a wistfulness in his voice.

'You want a written invitation?' she clucked. 'Sure you're invited.'

He hurts – being estranged from his family this way. Especially on a holiday like Thanksgiving. It's going to be strange – having turkey dinner in Mom's tiny apartment instead of at the condo. But that's another life.

Claudia spent the time before she was to meet Jill in the routine Sunday chores. Vacuuming, dusting, doing the week's laundry. Her mind constantly focusing on Michael.

Was this latest horror dumped on him by his ex-wife the death knell for their own relationship? But why should that come between Michael and her? she asked herself defiantly. Their being together was no financial drain on him.

Is his ex-wife – Lisa – playing him for a sucker? Seven thousand dollars for a medical test? Shouldn't Michael question this?

Immediately she felt guilty at her suspicions. A friend of Todd's had talked about a test her mother was scheduled to take that cost that much – a cardiac test not covered by health insurance. But her father was the CEO of a major corporation.

This morning, she guessed, Michael would be at the store. He'd want to see for himself the reception their mini-cookbook was receiving. He'd check on the story hour on the children's floor. The full-page ad in the Sunday *Times* had given substantial space to both the mini-cookbook and the story hour.

A glance at the clock told her it was time to head for the Lyric to meet Jill for brunch. She was touched that Jill made this effort to have brunch with her every Sunday. If not, Jill would probably sleep into the afternoon, she thought tenderly.

She entered the restaurant just as a booth was being vacated it, rushed to snare it. Jill wasn't here yet. Moments later a friendly waitress brought her a cup of decaf. She was being recognized as a 'regular,' she realized. Establishing roots in a new life.

'You expect your friend?' the waitress asked. Her smile warm.

154

'My daughter,' Claudia told her. 'Yes.'

Minutes later Jill strode through the door. Her eyes searching for her mother. Claudia held up a hand. Jill darted to join her.

'Hi, Mom.'

'Hi, darling.' *Why does Jill always look at me that way when we first meet each other? As though she's fearful I'm falling apart.*

'I can't believe it's almost Thanksgiving.' Jill shook her head in rejection. 'Time just runs away.'

Claudia chuckled. 'You're not supposed to say that at your age.'

'How're you doing?'

'Good. It was great being rescued from the selling floor.' She hesitated. 'I invited Michael for Thanksgiving, too. My boss,' she reminded. Hadn't she told Jill she might do that? 'Our two loners.'

'You said you might invite him,' Jill recalled. 'He's single, you said.'

'Divorced.' *Why is Jill looking at me with that quizzical expression?*

'He's got a thing for you,' Jill pounced delightedly. 'You like him!'

Claudia debated an instant. 'I guess the answer is "yes", to both.' Jill wouldn't disapprove – yet she felt awkward in this admission. 'But it isn't going anywhere – he has problems with his ex-wife—'

'Like what?' Jill demanded.

Claudia explained the situation. 'I know it sounds absurd – but Michael is caught in a bad situation. That insane divorce settlement.'

'So he's having financial problems. Why should that affect his having a relationship?'

'He's always fighting to be able to meet his commitments. To keep the money rolling in. He worries about – about distractions.'

'That's ridiculous,' Jill protested. 'He has a right to have a life of his own.'

'We're not having a relationship,' Claudia said quickly. 'Just a – a one-day-at-a-time thing. He's a very special person, Jill—'

'And his bitchy ex-wife is using him like crazy. How does he know she needs all this special care?' Jill exuded skepticism.

'She's been an invalid for years,' Claudia said after a moment. 'It's one of those things.'

But later – after they'd had brunch and Jill had taken off – Claudia asked herself if Jill was right. Was Lisa using Michael? How would he know? He never saw her. He was so ethical, so determined to do what was right. Was Lisa playing him for a sucker?

No, I want to think that Jill is right because that would open the way for Michael and me. But life isn't that simple. People get caught in ghastly situations.

Thirty-Three

After brunch with Jill, Claudia walked up to the store. Faintly self-conscious at this effort on a Sunday. The store had opened about fifteen minutes ago, she realized as she walked inside. She was astonished – and delighted – that the main floor was already heavily populated.

Her face lighted when she approached the elevator area and saw the table laden with their Thanksgiving mini-cookbooks and huge trays piled high with pumpkin cookies. Clusters of women were reaching for cookbook and cookies. Great, she thought with relief. At moments she'd been fearful that the project had smacked more of volunteer women's groups than of a major department store.

All afternoon and evening she fought against an urge to call Michael. To talk with him. Instinct warned her against this. He needed time alone.

On Monday morning she arrived at the store early as usual. Aching to see Michael after the traumatic weekend. Would this latest demand by Lisa derail Michael from trying to have a life of his own? And always in a corner of her mind these past few days was the fear that Michael would be sent out to Scottsdale to set up what he was calling a glorified specialty shop.

Entering their suite she heard Michael's voice in impassioned conversation behind the closed door of his office. On the phone, she pinpointed. Had he called Lisa in protest? No, Michael wouldn't do that. He was arguing with someone in the Chicago office, she surmised. Something to do with the proposed Scottsdale store?

At minutes before 9 a.m. Michael emerged from his office. He gazed at her cubicle, waved a greeting, then crossed to Dolores.

'I'll be away for about an hour,' he told her, 'in case there are calls.'

'Sure, boss,' Dolores flipped. 'I'll keep the wolves at bay.'

He was headed for his bank, Claudia guessed. To put in a loan application. With his business background he'd have no problems. *But he doesn't need another bill to pay every month.*

She tried to focus on the work at hand. That was difficult this morning. Thank God, Thanksgiving Day was just three days away. It would be so good to have a leisurely day with Michael. He said he'd be over early to help with the cooking. Larry wouldn't be upset that there'd be two strangers at the dinner table, would he?

Larry said he'd be arriving about noon, she recalled. He could grab a nap before they sat down to dinner. She'd told Jill not to worry about getting to the apartment early – just to be sure to be there in time to sit down at the table. She'd be bringing Chris with her.

157

Claudia's face softened as she visualized Thanksgiving morning. Just Michael and her in the kitchen. It would seem so right. She ached for more than a 'one day at a time' relationship. She and Michael needed each other on a full-time basis.

Michael returned in less than an hour. He stopped by Claudia's cubicle with a wan smile.

'No trouble at the bank,' he told her. 'Lisa will have her check by the end of the week.' His face inscrutable. 'Oh, about Thanksgiving dinner. What can I bring – besides our secret second dessert?'

'Just yourself,' she said softly. 'And come early. We'll have breakfast before we start with dinner.'

'Great.' His eyes making love to her. 'The reception for the Thanksgiving cookbook was fine – and for the cookies.' He paused, seeming all at once abashed. 'I popped in yesterday afternoon to see what kind of response they were getting.'

Claudia chuckled. 'I walked up after brunch with Jill,' she confessed. 'They were moving well.'

Claudia knew the three days before Thanksgiving would drag. On Wednesday she left the office minutes before 6 p.m. – a rarity in these past weeks. Michael was in a meeting. Dolores, too, was packing up for the day.

'Hey, you're working half a day,' Dolores joshed. 'Shopping for the big day?'

'That's right. My son's coming in from college for the weekend. And Jill is coming with a friend.' *She has that glint in her eyes again. Does she guess that Michael's coming for Thanksgiving dinner?*

'I'll be going to my sister's as usual,' Dolores told her. 'We'll eat too much, of course. Jane – my sister – wouldn't be happy if we didn't. And I'll bring home a care package to last a week.'

'Your sister lives in the city?' Claudia asked. Dolores never talked about her family. She'd envisioned Dolores as being a loner. But she couldn't have invited her to dinner if Michael was there, she reminded herself guiltily.

'Jane's lived in Brooklyn for twenty-three years. I make the trip out there about once a month – to see my sister and my two nieces and hear all the family gossip. Her husband I can't stand.' Dolores grimaced. 'But for Thanksgiving I can handle him.'

'Have a great one,' Claudia said and reached out to hug her. 'You deserve it.'

'You, too.' Dolores dug her purse from a desk drawer, collected her coat. 'Hang on a minute – I'll leave with you.'

By the time Claudia arrived at her supermarket, the aisles were packed. Piles of bags awaited pick-up by the delivery men. She rushed to shop. She should have done some of this earlier, she reproached herself.

Her shopping cart loaded, she waited in line at the check-out counter. The cashier was assuring the woman ahead of her that deliveries would be made within the hour. Waiting, she double-checked the list she'd made out earlier. Everything was here.

At the apartment she prepared herself a hasty dinner. Thank God for the George Foreman grill, she thought. Her chicken cutlet would be done in four minutes. A yam just needed to be heated in the toaster-oven. Stir-fried mixed vegetables would cook while the cutlet was on the grill.

She'd vacuumed and dusted Saturday morning. That would have to do for tomorrow. She'd put on a CD, have dinner, and wait for the delivery man. Despite her strict budget, she decided on a five-dollar tip. Those poor guys worked so hard for so little. How did they feel about walking into well-furnished, middle-class apartments when they were forced to live in slums?

She was midway through her dinner – eaten on a tray in the living room – when she suddenly remembered that she hadn't told Larry that Michael and Chris would be here for Thanksgiving dinner.

She put aside the tray, hurried to call him, got the answering machine that served Larry and his roommates.

'Hi, Larry,' she said lightly. 'I forgot to tell you we'll be having guests for Thanksgiving dinner. Jill's friend Chris and my boss Michael Walsh. It seemed the nice thing to do, since neither had a place to go. Drive carefully tomorrow – there'll be a lot of people on the road.' Larry had said he was borrowing the car of one of his apartment-sharers – the one who was flying to Bermuda to spend the four-day holiday with his vacationing parents.

Now she was fighting misgivings. Would Larry look at Michael and know she was emotionally involved with him? So soon after the divorce. Would Larry think she'd fallen for the first man who gave her a second glance?

Michael understands the situation. We'll play it cool. Thanksgiving dinner will be a lovely time.

Thirty-Four

Claudia awoke a little past 7 a.m. – after a night of broken slumber. Her mind instantly assaulted by a flood of questions. Will Larry be unhappy at having strangers at Thanksgiving dinner? Will Michael feel uncomfortable in Jill and Larry's company? Will Larry have a rough time finding a parking spot? *I should have told him to take the car straight to the garage around the corner.*

Enough of this – get out of bed. There was much to do this morning. She should have made the pumpkin pie last night, she berated herself. Would one package of cranberries be enough for five? Would one loaf of bread be enough for the turkey dressing? Oh, this was absurd, she scolded herself – rushing to shower and prepare for the day. There'd be one more person for dinner than in other years. Nobody would go hungry. *It's going to be a lovely day. I want Jill and Larry to get to know Michael.*

Standing under the body-pounding spray of the shower, she felt her head begin to clear. This was just a holiday dinner with two guests joining the family. No reason to feel uptight. She'd handled dinner parties for a dozen.

Would the kids be upset that Todd wasn't with them this year? He hadn't been with them last year either. No, he wouldn't enter their thoughts. Both were furious with him, vowed never to talk to him again.

She prayed that Jill and Larry would like Michael – but it wasn't as though she was introducing them to a prospective stepfather. She knew – any future for Michael and her was unlikely. And yet she rebelled at this thought.

Out of the shower she dressed for the day – remembering that she'd told Michael to come early and they'd have breakfast together. In the overheated apartment – a situation that seemed to inflict the entire five boroughs, whether in luxury apartments or city projects – she decided to dress casually. Wear jeans and a red tee-shirt – and sneakers.

In the kitchen she fortified herself with a cup of Earl Grey and a toasted English, then added the extension to the dinner table so that it would accommodate five. Set the table – know that was ready. She glanced at the clock. It was a few minutes before 8 a.m. Why hadn't she set a specific time with Michael? He'd be anxious about arriving too early.

Subconsciously listening for the intercom to announce Michael's arrival, she ground coffee beans, put up the coffee maker. The phone was a noisy intrusion in the morning quiet. She rushed to pick up.

'Hello.'

'Am I calling too early?' Michael was solicitous.

'I've been up for an hour. Come on over now – we'll have breakfast and then settle down to work.' She managed a festive air. Poor Michael, who'd endured so many cheerless Thanksgivings.

'I made the grasshopper pie last night – I hope it's okay—'

'I'm sure it's great. Come. Coffee's up already.'

161

Off the phone, she brought out eggs, whipped them into lightness, debated about omelet fillings, settled on low-fat Swiss cheese. They wouldn't be sitting down to dinner for hours – breakfast should be filling. Now she remembered an unused baked Idaho in the fridge. Home fries, she decided – requiring just a spray of oil in a non-stick pan. Orange juice from a container – no oranges available for fresh squeezed.

Ten minutes later Michael was at the door. He clutched a carton, which she assumed held the grasshopper pie.

'No sweat finding a cab this morning – not this early.' His eyes moved about the comfortably furnished living room with approval, sniffed the aroma of freshly brewed coffee. 'Hazelnut,' he identified and Claudia nodded.

'Let me put the pie away and we'll have breakfast.' *It feels so right to have Michael here.* 'We won't be eating until around two—'

He grinned, slid out of his thinsulate jacket, draped it about a chair in the dining area.

As though he's lived here for ages.

'Lots of work to do.'

I'm so glad I didn't dress up – I knew the kids wouldn't. And Michael looks so relaxed in chinos and plaid flannel shirt.

They sat down to breakfast with a mutual recognition that this was a very special occasion. While they ate, Michael focused on dinner preparations.

He's so organized.

'Oh, I brought my flavor injector along,' he said. 'It's in my jacket pocket.' He reached around to find it.

'That sounds like something from a science fiction novel—' Claudia's eyes lit with laughter as he laid it on the table.

'It creates magic,' he explained with a conspiratorial air. 'We'll give the turkey a jolt of bourbon.'

Claudia was startled. 'I don't know if we have bourbon—'

'We do.' He reached into another pocket to produce a miniature bottle.

162

With breakfast dishes stacked they tackled dinner preparations. Each delighted when one introduced some culinary trick new to the other. The pumpkin pie was in the oven. The turkey standing by to replace it in fifty-five minutes. The dressing an exotic concoction that Michael had devised through the years.

'We'll add the yams later,' Michael said. 'Do the salad and cranberry sauce just before we plan to sit down.' His eyes clung to hers with a hopeful question. 'Nobody will be arriving for quite a while?'

'No,' she whispered.

'Then let's not waste this precious time.' He pulled her close. 'I wish today could go on forever.'

'I'll put the chain on the door,' she said unsteadily. 'Not that Larry will show up for another hour. And I'll take any bet that Jill and Chris will arrive minutes before we sit down to dinner.'

Arm in arm they walked into the bedroom, closed the door as though to shut out the rest of the world. Claudia's heart pounded as Michael reached to pull her to him.

Oh yes, this is a perfect Thanksgiving Day.

Thirty-Five

By 12:45 – with dinner makings under control – Claudia and Michael sat down in the living room with fresh mugs of coffee and contented smiles. Michael had been regaling her with stories of his two Thanksgiving dinners while in the Peace Corps.

'I'd told the families with whom I'd been living about Thanksgiving Day back home,' he wound up. 'And since no turkeys were available there, one Thanksgiving dinner featured a whole pig – which I suspected had been stolen and slaughtered during the night. The second family served a strange bird I was told was pheasant – though I suspect otherwise. Still, both families were determined to make their Peace Corps boarder feel at home.' His eyes glowed in recall. 'It was a great experience.'

Only now did Claudia realize that Larry was late – or later than he'd anticipated.

'So Larry's running a little late,' Michael soothed, noting her frequent glances towards the door. 'You know what driving's like on a major holiday.'

Moments later the doorbell rang. Claudia leaped to her feet. Her face radiant.

'That's Larry!' It was too early for Jill and Chris. She'd told the doorman the three of them were expected, to send them directly upstairs.

She pulled the door wide. 'Darling, you're late – I was beginning to worry.' She reached joyously to embrace him.

'First, the traffic was wild. Big stretches where every car just sat. Then I had trouble finding a parking spot.' His sigh was eloquent. 'I thought it would be a breeze on a big holiday. I guess a lot of people are just staying home instead of taking trips. I can't believe the cost of gas.' He glanced past her towards Michael. His smile warm. 'Hi—'

'Michael, this is my baby,' she crooned, and Larry shook his head in good-humored reproach. 'Larry, this is Michael – my boss at the store.'

'Hi—' Michael reached out a hand to Larry's. 'You'd probably like some coffee to tide you over till dinner.'

'Hey, right. I'll need something to keep me awake.' He turned to his mother. 'It was a big night off-campus – I worked till curfew, then got up before seven.'

'Then go into the bedroom and take a nap,' she ordered. 'I'll call you when we're ready to sit down to dinner.'

'That'll be great—' He stifled a yawn. 'Give me ten

minutes warning—' But he was already moving towards the bedroom.

Clock-watching again – because Jill and Chris had not arrived – Claudia hovered beside Michael at the range as he added a bit of orange zest to the cranberry sauce – where he'd instructed her to use orange juice rather than water.

'Of course, there's an atrocious amount of sugar in this pan,' he acknowledged, 'but how often do we serve cranberry sauce?'

The doorbell rang again. 'That's Jill and Chris.' She hurried to the door – conscious of a flicker of anxiety. She felt as though she knew Chris, but this would be their first personal encounter.

'We're early,' Jill chortled while embracing her mother. 'Chris's good influence.'

'I'm so glad you could come, Chris.' She extended a hand in welcome.

'Thanks for having me. I'd be calling in for Chinese or running down to the neighborhood McDonald's.' His smile was charismatic, Claudia decided. 'Oh, I brought a bottle of bubbly – I hope that's okay?'

'It's great.' She reached to take the parcel from Chris. 'Thank you.'

'Domestic—' A note of apology in Chris's voice.

'We believe in "buying American",' Claudia said lightly.

'Let me put it in the fridge to chill,' Michael said, then appeared disconcerted.

'Good idea,' Claudia told him and handed over the bottle. *He was afraid he sounded too proprietary.*

'Did Larry get down?' Jill asked, removing her jacket and gesturing to Chris to do the same.

'He's asleep in the bedroom. He worked last night.' Jill knew about Larry's bar job. 'Is the slave mill letting you off tomorrow?' Claudia's smile indulgent as they settled themselves in the living room.

'Yes and no—' Jill was somber. 'The offices are closed, but I'll go in for three or four hours—' Chris uttered a disbelieving grunt. 'Okay, maybe for five or six hours.'

They've developed a warm relationship fast. He seems awfully nice. 'I explained to Michael that you don't like pumpkin pie,' Claudia told Jill.

'Wow,' Chris clucked. 'That's unpatriotic.'

'Anyhow, Michael forgives you – he's made a second dessert.'

'Oh?' Jill's eyebrows rose in interest. 'What?'

'You'll have to wait.' Claudia was firm.

'This is a man who cooks big time.' Chris nodded in respect as Michael rejoined them. 'The best I can do is concoct a great hamburger. Of course,' Chris admitted, 'Jill insists I make it a chicken burger.'

'That's Mom's influence. When she cooks, you know it's going to be healthful.' Jill giggled in recall. 'When I was in high school – out west – she blew her stack when she found out what made up the school lunch menu. She was a one-woman powerhouse to redesign what we ate for lunch.' Jill glowed with pride.

I never knew Jill was pleased – I thought she was kind of embarrassed at my involvement. But all those fatty foods – and the loads of sugar! I had to do something.

'I started cooking over twenty years ago,' Michael reminisced. 'It was relaxing. Of course, in those days it wasn't considered exactly macho.'

'Look at all the great male chefs,' Chris pointed out. 'Then and now.'

'I never had any great ambition to be a chef,' Michael admitted

'What did you want to do?' Chris probed good-humoredly.

Michael gazed at him – disconcerted for a moment. 'When I was fresh out of college, I'd thought – unrealistically – about opening a restaurant.' His eyes lighted. 'Not just a neighborhood luncheonette or some fast-food deal that could expand into a chain. I had this crazy idea about operating a small restaurant geared to diners who expect gourmet food – but have a keen eye for what's healthful. I'd like to plan the meals, experiment with recipes – and let a crew carry them out.' A hint of self-consciousness in his chuckle.

'Today's dinner won't be totally traditional,' Claudia warned. 'Not when Michael laced the turkey with bourbon, added his secret ingredients to the dressing. And, Jill, you'll love the second dessert.'

'Who did something with the yams that goes way beyond the traditional marshmallows?' Michael challenged. *Don't look at me that way, Michael. The others will know how we feel about each other.*

A timer went off in the kitchen. Michael rose to his feet. 'Dinner will be on the table in ten minutes.'

Claudia followed him. 'Jill, wake Larry. Tell him to splash some water on his face and join us.'

'Sure, Mom.' Jill hesitated. 'I don't think we have champagne glasses, but—'

'Hold the champagne for after dinner,' Claudia called over her shoulder. 'The ultimate conclusion for Thanksgiving dinner.'

Claudia and Michael made a joyful production of serving dinner. *Neither Larry nor Jill were upset that their father wasn't here,* she told herself with relief. Chris seemed to be enjoying himself, she thought compassionately. How awful not to be speaking with his family. And Michael was keeping everybody amused with stories of his two Thanksgiving dinners while in the Peace Corps.

'Of course, that was a hell of a long time ago,' he mused, 'but times like that you remember.'

'What did you do with these yams?' Chris asked, reaching for a second serving. 'Cool.'

Amazed that Chris was interested in recipes, Claudia explained – with amusing commentary from Michael. All through dinner Chris had seemed intrigued by the off-beat treatment of each dish. And it made for light, lively conversation.

'You know—' Chris paused, squinted in thought. 'I'll bet you two –' he glanced from Claudia to Michael – 'could write a great cookbook. Adding in all those flip remarks you each make.'

167

After a startled moment Claudia and Michael broke into laughter.

'Spoken as a member of the literary world,' Jill drawled. 'This guy lives publishing.'

'I'm working my way up from the bottom,' he reminded her. 'And publishing is an ideas business. But cookbooks are big business – and people are excited about eating healthy—' He squinted in thought. 'Or is it healthful?'

'Chris, this is supposed to be your day off,' Jill admonished. 'Forget about publishing.'

'My old man wanted me to go into investment banking,' Chris jeered. 'I keep telling Jill: "Get the hell out of investment banking – you hate it."'

'I don't hate the paycheck.' Jill's smile was defiant.

Is Chris truly gay? Not the way he looks at Jill. His sister – who said he was – had been watching re-runs of Three's Company. *And he was desperate for an apartment.*

'When's dessert?' Larry demanded, glancing from his mother to Michael. 'Jill woke me up with the promise of two desserts.'

'Two desserts coming up,' Michael confirmed. 'But let's clear the table first.'

Larry suspects there's something special between Michael and me, doesn't he? Michael doesn't realize it – but he's more host than guest. And it feels so right.

Thirty-Six

Larry sprawled on the living-room sofa and watched evening TV reports on the major football games of the day. Claudia focused on reading her current issue of *Vanity Fair*. She felt mellow. Relaxed. This had been a beautiful day. In a corner of her mind she'd been dreading it. The first Thanksgiving Day in the family's new life.

'Come on, it was cool!' Larry talked back to the sports-caster on the TV screen, then smothered a wide yawn.

'Larry, any time you want to go to sleep, just run me out of the room,' Claudia told him. 'I'm going to read a bit, then go to sleep myself. Tomorrow's a work day.'

Larry pulled himself into a sitting position, regarded her with a blend of affection and respect. 'You're terrific, Mom. You're a real survivor.'

'We're doing better than millions of other families.' A certain defiance in her voice. So much uncertainty lay ahead. 'I suppose you'll sleep till noon tomorrow—'

'Yeah. I'm meeting a couple of guys from school who live in the city. We'll hang out together – and there's a party tonight and another tomorrow night.' His smile was apologetic.

'This is a mini-vacation, darling. Enjoy.'

'You won't mind if I don't show up for dinner?'

'Of course not. Pop in when you feel like it. The refrigerator will be loaded with leftovers. If you're hungry when you get home, check the fridge.'

'Sure, Mom. That's a good deal.'

He's relieved. I don't want him to feel he has to worry about me 'But let's have brunch together on Sunday before you hit the trail. You and I – and probably Jill. Okay?' What was important was that they'd been together today. A family.

She discarded her magazine, rose to her feet. 'I think I'll call it a night now – I keep early office hours. Let me get your bedding out of the hall closet. Open up the sofa when you're ready for bed.'

'Mom—' He hesitated. 'You like this job?'

'It's fine.' She opened the closet door, brought out pillows, sheets, a light blanket. 'I don't know that it'll last beyond the first of the year,' she admitted.

'Michael seems to be a good guy.' Questions in his eyes that he couldn't bring himself to voice, Claudia interpreted.

169

'As a boss he's top-notch.' *Don't rush – let Larry get used to Michael.* 'And he's become a good friend. We – we have a lot in common.'

But how long will Michael be a part of my life?

Claudia kept her movements quiet as she prepared for the working day. Larry lay sound asleep on the sofa-bed. *How nice to have him here this way.*

She avoided making breakfast – it would be noisy. Let Larry sleep. She'd pick up coffee and a low-fat muffin on the way to the store.

She walked out of the building into the morning cold, intensified by a sharp wind. She pulled her coat collar closer about her throat, quickened her steps. Still, she'd come to relish the walk from home to store. It gave her a sense of control to avoid mass transit.

She was aware of lighter traffic than usual. Many offices were closed for the long weekend. The stores expected heavy business today. She stopped at a coffee shop to pick up decaf and muffin. No line here this morning.

Approaching the store she remembered the Christmas windows were to be unveiled this morning. A crew still moved behind the concealing drapes, she suspected – tending to last-minute details.

She was surprised to find Dolores already at her desk.

'You're an early bird,' she joshed.

Dolores chuckled. 'It was matter of self-preservation.'

'Oh?' Claudia lifted an eyebrow.

'My sister and the kids insisted I spend the night. But I couldn't face breakfast with my brother-in-law. I escaped early – before he was up. How was your Thanksgiving?'

'Very pleasant. Both kids were with me.' She paused a moment. 'And Jill brought a friend.' *I can't say, 'Michael was with us, and that was lovely.'*

'Thanksgiving dinner was great,' Dolores acknowledged. 'I probably gained three pounds.' She winced, patted her waist-line. 'If I don't eat like a pig at holiday dinners, my sister's sure I hate what she served. Anyhow, I'm off the hook now till Christmas.'

'I don't want to think about Christmas yet.' *But it's close. Time just runs away.*

Claudia hung away her coat, glanced at the door to Michael's office. 'Is Michael in yet?'

'Why wouldn't he be?' Dolores's eyes were tender. 'I hope he had a decent Thanksgiving.'

Not until well into the morning did Claudia talk with Michael. He closed the door to the office when she came into the room.

'Yesterday was wonderful,' he said. 'I didn't want it to end.' But he seemed so somber.

She searched his eyes for a moment. 'What's bothering you, Michael?'

'I had a call this morning from Chicago. They seem to be serious about this Scottsdale store. They've asked me to go out there the weekend after next. Check out the town, talk with a couple of real estate agents. Damn it, why Scottsdale?' he demanded in frustration. 'Why can't I stay here? Or go back to running the White Plains store—'

Claudia fought for poise. 'Maybe Scottsdale isn't dense enough in population,' she ventured. 'You might have to hand in a negative report.'

His private phone line rang. He scowled, guessing – along with her – that this was Chicago calling again. He picked up. 'Hello, Michael Walsh.'

I don't want him to move to Scottsdale – or Los Angeles or anywhere else. I want to be able to see him – even on a 'one day at a time' basis.

Though her company was officially closed for the long weekend, Jill had been at her desk since minutes past 9 a.m. this Friday morning. Here and there other offices were occupied, though there was a funereal quietness on her floor. She ordered lunch sent in, ate with little appetite. By 5:30 p.m. she decided – with a touch of inner rebellion – to cut out. Enough already.

She phoned the company car service. This was a rotten time to find an empty cab. She'd go home, grab a nap, then order in dinner.

As had been happening at unwary moments all day, her mind wandered to the unexpectedly somber conversation with Chris when they'd come home last night. He'd seemed so convivial at dinner and the couple of hours afterwards when they'd remained at Mom's apartment. But home again, she realized he was miserable at being isolated from his family.

'Mom called me this morning – to wish me a happy Thanksgiving. But she won't concede Dad's wrong. Can't they both understand I'm a grown man – I have a right to make my own decisions? Mom wants me to call Dad, apologize. She said he'll talk to his friend again about taking me into his company. I don't want that, Jill.'

The car was waiting when she walked out of the building, whisked her home in ten minutes. Opening the apartment door, she saw Chris in the kitchen, was conscious of savory aromas. Onions frying, she identified.

'Hi,' Chris greeted her. 'I called you at the office, got your voicemail.' He grimaced. 'Why is it so hard to get a human voice in the business world? Anyhow, I figured you were on your way home and hungry. Like me.' He pointed to the two over-sized chicken burgers sitting before the grill.

'Ah yes, you can cook, too,' she drawled, sliding out of her jacket. Since this was an official holiday she'd gone to the office in jeans, turtleneck, and L.L. Bean jacket. 'What other hidden talents?'

He grinned, moving the burgers onto the grill. 'You'd be surprised.' She was startled by the glint in his eyes as they met hers. The atmosphere suddenly electric. 'Michael's not the only guy who cooks. But he's got more talent. Like your mom. That was a great dinner yesterday.'

'I'll set the table—' Jill reached into a cabinet for plates. *Why am I feeling this way?*

'Salad plates, too,' he instructed. 'We're having a huge salad.' He grinned. 'It's cool, the way you can buy salad in a bag –

172

all washed and ready to serve. I added a tomato and a cuke. Voilà – dinner.'

They moved about the kitchen – small for two, admittedly – in a pleasant silence, then settled themselves at the bistro table in the dining area. Biting into his onion-smothered chicken burger, Chris uttered sounds of appreciation. The tea kettle whistled on the range. Jill went to silence it, returned to the table. Tea could wait.

'Would you by any chance have a disposable photo of your mom?' Chris asked with studied casualness. 'And might she have a photo of Michael? From the office,' he added quickly.

Jill stared in suspicion. 'What are you up to?'

'You know how I was talking about your mom and Michael doing a cookbook? Well—'

'Chris, they didn't agree to anything like that,' she broke in.

'I know,' he soothed. 'But I'm thinking through how I would approach an editor with an idea for a book.' His smile was sheepish. 'This is my learning process. A dry run. I'm trying to present the whole picture. Your mom's great looking – that's a plus. And Michael's good looking, too.' Jill was startled by his dreamy-eyed gaze into space. 'Really charismatic.'

'Chris, Michael isn't gay.'

'Neither am I,' Chris said – and froze. 'Oh, man, I cut my throat, didn't I?'

'I wondered about that,' Jill conceded. Their eyes clinging.

'It's been killing me – having you think I was gay. When I look at you, and all I want to do is hold you in my arms.'

'Let's don't rush this,' she cautioned unsteadily.

'Slow and easy,' he agreed, but one hand reached across the table for hers. Chicken burgers and salad forgotten. 'Oh, God, I'm glad you know. It's been such hell.'

'And this business about Mom and Michael,' she probed. 'It's just been a game?'

'No.' His smile was dazzling. 'I think they have great

potential. If I can bring them in – and they're a big success – I'll move up the ladder fast.'

'Chris Taylor, are you just using me?' Jill was indignant.

'Baby, I'm thinking of our future. I see us as a lifetime team.' Unexpectedly he grinned. 'And I won't just be acquiring my perfect soulmate – but a mother-in-law to die for.'

'Slow and easy,' she reminded him. *Am I out of my mind? Can we handle this?*

Thirty-Seven

Michael glanced at his watch. It was almost seven o'clock. No real reason to hang around here – he'd be in tomorrow to take care of loose ends. No need to keep Claudia plodding away at what she could handle tomorrow.

He left his office, crossed to Claudia's cubicle. Dolores had left an hour ago.

'Let's call it a day,' he told Claudia, managed a chuckle. 'Your kids probably think I'm a slave driver.'

'Jill and Larry know I love my job.' Her eyes said, 'I love you.'

'I was thinking – maybe we could have dinner together. Unless you have something planned with the kids,' he added.

'Larry's carousing with college friends. He warned me he wouldn't be home until late. And I won't be seeing Jill until Sunday brunch.'

'My kitchen is kind of barren. We'll stop off to shop at—'

'Come to my apartment,' she broke in. 'The fridge is loaded with leftovers.' She glowed in anticipation. 'One of the lovely perks of big holiday dinners.'

'Sounds great.' His face softened. 'I remember when I was

a kid – the Fridays after Thanksgiving dinner when we used to make a ceremony of raiding the fridge for dinner. And my mother always used to find a second pumpkin pie in the freezer—' He gazed into space. 'Did I ever tell you? My mother and Dad died within five months of each other. They were the only family I had. That's when I went into the Peace Corps. For twenty-seven months the Peace Corps was my family.'

'I always wished I had a brother or sister,' Claudia told him. 'I was glad that I had a son and a daughter.' She paused. 'Larry says he won't be home until late,' she reiterated, 'but he might pop in earlier.' Her eyes met his in wistful apology.

'Note taken.' His smile was wry. He understood this was to be a casual evening. Rough, when he ached already to make love. *What about Scottsdale? Can I ask her to go out there with me?*

'Let me turn off the computer, and we can take off.' A festive air about her now. 'We didn't quite finish Chris's bottle of champagne yesterday. For dessert what about strawberries drizzled with champagne?'

'We'll pick up strawberries on the way to your place.' He reached for her coat, held it for her. *Claudia's become such an important part of my life. I don't want to put distance between us.*

Later – standing in Claudia's kitchen – they radiated a convivial air as they inventoried the contents of the refrigerator, made choices, settled themselves at the dining table. Both conscious that Larry might have a last-minute change of plans, pop in at any moment.

Michael—' Claudia seemed in some inner debate. 'Is there any way you could tell the company you want to remain in this area?'

'No.' He was terse. 'I don't know how they'd react.' He considered the situation for a moment. 'There's a slight possibility that I'll check out Scottsdale and come up with a negative response. But there's still the possibility the big wheels will decide to keep Los Angeles open. I can't make waves – I need that large check every payday.'

'Let's don't think about that tonight.' Claudia was determinedly optimistic. 'Maybe a miracle will happen.'

The weekend had sped past, Claudia thought as she stood under the shower on Monday morning. She'd seen Larry for brief periods on Friday and Saturday. On Sunday she and Larry met with Jill for brunch at the Lyric. After brunch Larry took off for school.

She and Michael had lengthy phone conversations on Saturday and Sunday evenings. He recoiled from the prospect of being in the same town as his ex-wife – though it wasn't likely that they'd run into each other, she had kept reassuring him.

He's fearful, too, of finding Scottsdale is a great town for a Miller's branch. But if not there, there's still the possibility that he'll be shipped out to L.A.

As usual this morning, the apartment was overheated. But a quick check of the TV weather news warned the day was bleak, winter-cold, with a threat of snow. *'A possible accumulation of two to four inches by nightfall.'* She adored snow – out of the city.

She dawdled over breakfast – in this weather she'd take the Third Avenue bus uptown, walk across to Fifth Avenue. And all the while she was conscious of a new year that might not include Michael. And sometime in January – with her sublet approaching its end – she must start searching for a new apartment. She shuddered, remembering New York's escalating rents.

Arriving at the store, she flinched at the sight of the ornate Christmas decorations that emblazoned the main floor. This morning they seemed to taunt her. She rushed to the comfort of Michael's suite.

Dolores hadn't arrived yet. The door to Michael's office was open. Hearing her arrival, he came to the door, called to her as she hung away her coat.

'Claudia—' A touch of urgency in his voice.

'Hi,' she said softly, walking into his office.

'I hate Sundays.' He reached to pull her close. 'Because that's a day I don't see you.'

'We'll have to do something about that—' It felt so good, to be here with him this way.

'Go out to Scottsdale with me next weekend,' he pleaded. 'It's just for a weekend – but it could be a slice of heaven. We'll fly out Friday evening, fly back Sunday afternoon. I'll have to spend much of Saturday with the real estate people,' he acknowledged, 'but there'll be lots of time for us. Two beautiful nights—'

'I don't know,' she whispered. Unnerved at the prospect.

'Why not?' he challenged. 'Let us have that time together. Just the two of us – away from the world.'

'I have to think about it,' she stalled. *But Michael's right. Why can't we have that? Jill won't be upset. Larry's back at school. I'm a free woman.* 'Yes!' Her face was luminous. 'Let us have that.'

'I'll make our flight arrangements myself,' he decided. So her presence would not be noted. 'I'll have Dolores reserve a car rental at the Phoenix airport. You'll drive me to my first morning appointment with a real estate broker.' He paused. 'You have a driver's license?'

'Oh, yes.' She hadn't expected to be using it.

'You leave me there and take off to play the tourist bit. I have three appointments – all within short walking distance of one another. I figure I should be through by five o'clock. I'll take a cab to our hotel. I'll have Dolores reserve a suite – in my name – at the Phoenician. Hopefully we can get a reservation – this is the very beginning of the high season.'

'That could be a problem,' Claudia warned, caught up in this unexpected adventure. 'But there'll be other hotels—'

'But to stay at the Phoenician is a magnificent experience. Every guest is treated like visiting royalty.' Michael's face clouded for a moment. 'I had to go out to Scottsdale for the closing on Lisa's condo. To pay all the bills,' he explained drily. 'She insisted we stay at the Phoenician – she and her nurse-companion in one suite, I in their least expensive single

177

room.' He winced in recall. 'That was the last time I saw her.'

'You won't see her this time,' Claudia reminded gently.

Michael made an effort now to discard hateful memories. 'But Scottsdale is such a magnificent town – set there at the base of Camelback Mountain. I was there only for twenty-four hours,' he admitted, 'but it was long enough to marvel at the spectacular views.'

'We'll only be there for the weekend, but what about clothes?' Claudia asked. 'It'll be warmer than New York, I suspect.'

'Oh yes! The weather is fantastic. It might drop down to forty degrees in early morning and evening – but then the temperature soars into the low seventies. You'll dress for mild winter for breakfast, then start shedding. Around mid-afternoon, you'll start adding for warmth. And it rarely rains, people there told me. I promise you, my love,' he said tenderly, 'it's going to be a very special time for us.'

Lying sleepless well past midnight, Claudia was conscious of errant thoughts. An earlier conversation with Jill – when they'd talked about Michael's invalid ex-wife – ricocheted in her mind at regular intervals:

'His bitchy ex-wife is using him like crazy. How does he know she needs all this special care? He never sees her.'

Claudia's heart began to race. Was Lisa playing Michael for a sucker? How would he know? She was out there in Scottsdale – two thousand miles away. He hadn't seen her, he said, since the closing on her condo.

Claudia searched her mind for answers. She wanted to think that Lisa was using him, she accused herself. Because then nothing would stand between Michael and her.

Is Lisa playing him for a sucker? All right, it's a long shot – but it could be true. I'll be out there in Scottsdale. Use that time! Track down Michael's ex-wife – discover if she is a fraud.

178

Thirty-Eight

Now Claudia spent the working hours on extensive research on Scottsdale. Its density, the average income of full-time residents, the major shopping area, the line-up of shops in the Miller price range, the local tax structure. She spent much time on long-distance calls – to the Scottsdale Chamber of Commerce, the local public library.

In a late evening phone call Claudia told Jill about the prospective weekend in Scottsdale.

'That's cool,' Jill approved. 'You need a break.'

The following evening she spoke with Larry – guilty at her subterfuge.

'I'll be out at Shirley's house from Friday night until Sunday evening. Let me give you her number in the rare event you need to reach me,' she said lightly. Shirley had been briefed. They both doubted that Larry would call – but if he did, Shirley would manage.

And each day she grappled with the problem of how to check up on the actual status of Lisa's health. A casual question had elicited the fact that Lisa had kept her married name after the divorce. Calling Scottsdale telephone information, she elicited the phone number of a Lisa Walsh. Good, she told herself with satisfaction, she'd be able to find an address in the Scottsdale phone directory.

She would camp in front of Lisa's condo from the moment she left Michael at his first appointment until she drove back to the hotel in the late afternoon, she plotted. Somewhere in the course of the day Lisa would emerge.

How would she recognize Lisa when she surfaced? She wouldn't be wearing a sign saying 'I'm Lisa Walsh.' *Some time in the course of the day she will emerge, won't she? But how will I recognize her?*

Growing desperate as Friday approached, she plotted to play the curious lover.

'Michael,' she began as they prepared to leave for the day on Thursday, 'was Lisa – is Lisa – a beautiful woman?' Her smile was wistful, as though she feared not stacking up to her predecessor.

'I suppose you'd call her attractive,' Michael said after a moment. 'On the outside.'

'I don't suppose you have any photos – snapshots – of her?' Guilty at playing games with Michael, yet desperate to be able to recognize Lisa. *Is she truly an invalid – or will a normal, healthy woman walk out of that condo?* 'I'd so much like to see a photo.'

'No photos.' Michael was terse for a moment. 'Wait – there's the photo album she kept. I remember noticing she'd left it behind when she moved to Scottsdale. It's packed in a closet where I store the stuff I mean to throw out,' he recalled wryly. 'It's been sitting there for years – while I've waited for free time to clear it out.'

'Bring a snapshot with you tomorrow,' she pleaded with a note of apology. 'I'd just like to see it.'

'Sure,' he said, his smile indulgent. 'Then we'll dump it in the garbage.'

Friday morning Claudia awoke with instant awareness that in a dozen hours she and Michael would be aboard a flight to Phoenix, where they'd rent a car and drive the ten miles to Scottsdale. A last-minute cancellation at the Phoenician had assured them a reservation.

'A suite,' Michael had told her with relish. 'Courtesy of my expense account.'

Michael would bring his weekender to the store this morning, Claudia reminded herself. Mindful of their flight time, they'd leave the office very early, cab to her apartment to pick up her luggage. Their flight would leave at 7:10 p.m. from La Guardia, would arrive in Phoenix at Phoenix International at 9:30 p.m. Phoenix time. In New York it would be 12:30 a.m.

Under the shower Claudia asked herself if Dolores would be curious when she, too, left the office unfamiliarly early. She'd told Dolores she was going out to visit Shirley for the weekend, taking off early since Michael would be away from the office.

Dolores is suspicious – but she approves. She's a romantic at heart.

Claudia arrived at the office early as usual. She was suffused with conflicting emotions. Anticipation of an exquisite weekend with Michael. Fear that she might discover Lisa was all she claimed to be – which would mark the end of a dream.

Michael arrived minutes later, along with Dolores. The glint in Dolores's eyes said she was aware that this would be a special weekend for Michael and her, Claudia interpreted. But neither Dolores nor Michael could know her special project.

Closeted in Michael's office – presumably for a last-minute review of her research of Scottsdale – Claudia waited for a strategic moment to ask Michael about the photo of Lisa he'd promised to bring in this morning.

'How can I get any work done this morning?' he murmured, 'when in a few hours we'll be on our way to heaven?'

'Michael—' She struggled to sound casual. 'Did you bring the photo you promised?'

For a moment he stiffened in distaste. 'I brought it.' He reached for his attaché case, withdrew a manila envelope. 'Here's the collection. Look at them – then shred them,' he ordered.

Alone in her cubicle, she inspected the snapshots of Lisa. She would have been very pretty, Claudia thought, except for the petulant smile. She gazed intently at the several snapshots – intent on etching the image onto her memory. Then – ensuring that Dolores was unaware of this activity – she put each into the shredder.

181

The day moved faster than she'd expected. She met Fran for a quick lunch, parroted her story about spending the weekend with her friend Shirley on Long Island. In early afternoon – minutes apart – first Michael, then she left for the day. She sighed with relief when Michael signaled a cab to the curb.

In record time they arrived at La Guardia for the routine hassle that was part of flying. Refusing to become annoyed at the delays until they were settled in their first-class seats. Their plane lifted off. Michael reached for her hand.

'We're on our way to a slice of heaven,' he whispered.

Six hours later – minutes past 1 a.m. in New York, 10 p.m. in Scottsdale – they were in their car rental and en route to the Phoenician, sprawling over 250 acres in the Sonora Desert.

'We're almost there,' Michael announced with an air of anticipation. 'It sits there at the foot of Camelback Mountain with glorious views of the Valley of the Sun. At night you see the lights of the city.'

Michael swung off Jokake Boulevard, turned left into the Phoenician's grounds.

'Oh, how gorgeous!' Claudia gazed in delight as they drove up to the hotel.

The huge marbled lobby with its towering fountains, the awesome collection of authentic Dutch paintings were impressive.

'The paintings are said to be worth eight million,' Michael murmured as they were escorted to their suite.

Their suite – its furniture the finest of light and airy rattan – was the height of luxury, provided its own private patio. The elegant marble bathroom was huge.

'This is larger than my apartment back home,' Claudia said lightly when they were alone. 'Such elegance!'

'Shall we call room service?' Michael asked. 'Dinner on the plane wasn't exactly a gourmet experience. I remember when I was about twelve, and Mom and Dad took me for a month in London and Switzerland. We didn't travel first class,' he said with wry humor, 'but I was fascinated by the fabulous trays that swept past through the economy section into first class. That's disappeared these days.'

'No,' she said, her eyes eloquent. 'We have other things in mind.'

'I wish this could be forever,' he murmured, reaching for her.

'Oh yes,' she agreed. *I feel so young, so carefree – so in love. I never dreamt it could happen to me.*

Later – lying in the curve of Michael's arms in the multi-pillowed king-sized bed – Claudia asked herself if she could go through with her intended pursuit of Michael's ex-wife. Could she face the anguish of discovering Lisa was the physical wreck she claimed to be?

But maybe Lisa is a fraud. I owe it to Michael and me to find out the truth. I can do this. But if she isn't, it'll be the end of a dream.

Thirty-Nine

Sleeping soundly, Claudia and Michael lay tangled together on their king-sized bed. The early morning chill alleviated by the whisper of heat provided for such mornings. The alarm on Michael's travel clock shattered the stillness with a modest wake-up call.

Claudia stirred, ignoring for a moment the summons that continued. How marvelous to wake up this way – in Michael's arms. But reality set in. She reached across to silence the alarm clock.

'Am I dreaming – or is this real?' Michael murmured, his arms tightening about her.

'You have a ten o'clock appointment,' she reminded while his mouth nuzzled at her throat.

'That's almost two hours away—' He smothered a yawn. It had been past 3 a.m. – New York time – before they drifted off in sleep, she remembered. 'Ten minutes more,' he bargained, 'then we'll get up and shower. Together,' he decided. 'I feel like eighteen again.'

'When you were eighteen, did you shower with your girl of the night?' she challenged. 'I'm jealous.' *Is this me talking this way? Like eighteen.*

'I wish you could be my girl of every night,' he whispered. 'Dear God, do I wish that!'

They chose to have breakfast served on their private patio, luxuriated in the elegant service, the fine food, the breath-taking view. But their mood had become more somber. Claudia knew Michael dreaded the task that lay ahead. Of all the places in the world he was most eager to avoid, it was Scottsdale – because somewhere out there was Lisa.

'I'll play the tourist while you're busy with the brokers,' Claudia told Michael while they sipped fragrant black coffee. 'I bought this so-called entry-level-photographer type of digital camera. I'll take loads of shots. For posterity,' she said, managing a light laugh. *I don't want to think beyond this weekend.*

'Drive me over to the first broker's office, then you're on your own.' He reached across the table for her hand. 'I never guessed I could feel this way about anyone.'

Half an hour later – at the exact time of his first appoint-ment – Michael pulled up before his destination.

'You'll manage okay?' All at once he was solicitous. 'I'll give you the names of the brokers I'm seeing. If you have any problems, call me on the cellphone.'

Claudia's laugh was tender. 'Michael, I conducted a dozen guided tours as part of a volunteer group seven years ago. For charity. I've developed a great sense of direction.'

'I'll cab back to the hotel. I should be there no later than six,' he promised. 'We'll have dinner at Mary Elaine's.' One of the eleven restaurants and lounges on the Phoenician prem-ises, Claudia recalled. 'Probably the fanciest restaurant in the state.'

Claudia drove away – ostensibly to the first of the tourist high spots on her list. Her heart was pounding. This morning she'd managed to sneak a glance at a local telephone directory in their suite. She had the address of Lisa's condo – and a map of Scottsdale on the seat of the car. She headed now for Lisa's condo complex.

She sat in the parking area adjacent to the attractive, low-slung structure. A tightness in her throat. Willing herself to follow her plan. She reached for the cellphone, hit Lisa's numbers. She heard the rings. Was nobody home? Then a male voice came on the line. A young male voice, she noted subconsciously.

'Hello—'

'May I speak to Lisa Walsh, please.'

She heard the man on the other end of the line call out. 'Lisa, it's for you.'

'Ask who it is,' an imperious feminine voice ordered. *Lisa?*

'Who is this?' he inquired, seeming angry at this intrusion.

'My name is Carol Hollis,' Claudia improvised. 'I'm just back from an assignment in Afghanistan. I knew a Lisa Walsh over there – she said she lived in Scottsdale or Phoenix – I'm not sure which. I'm trying to catch up with her.' Despite the coolness of the morning, Claudia was perspiring.

As she spoke, she heard Lisa call to him in annoyance. 'Darling, tell her to stop wasting my time. Go out and bring the Jag around—'

'You've got the wrong person,' he said tersely and slammed down the receiver.

Who's the young-ish man whom Lisa called 'darling'? Not her nurse-companion. And she's driving a Jaguar?

Claudia reached for her camera, glanced about the outdoor parking area. Two Jaguars sat there. One of them belonged to Lisa? She glanced about, saw another car swing out of the indoor garage. A red Jaguar.

Don't muff this. Get a shot of Lisa – and of her young man.

The red Jaguar pulled up before the entrance to the building.

185

Claudia focused on the doorway. Each minute seemed an hour. A middle-aged couple in lively conversation emerged. Moments later a teenage boy with a dog. The young man at the wheel of the red Jaguar tapped impatiently on the wheel of the car. Where was Lisa? Then a tall blonde strode out, headed towards the car. Claudia tensed, straining for a clear view. Yes! *Lisa.* In tight white slacks, a red suede jacket over what appeared to be a white tee-shirt.

Claudia shot half a dozen photos of Lisa and her companion – at least fifteen years her junior. Now she pretended to be engrossed in her road map. But instinct told her they were unaware of her presence. Too wrapped up in each other. Was the $7,000 Lisa had demanded for a 'cardiac test' the down-payment on the Jaguar – or to cover a lengthy rental?

Claudia waited until the red Jaguar swung onto the road, then grimly pursued. Here was proof that Lisa was not an invalid! She followed them doggedly – keeping another car always between them. Go after more proof, she ordered herself – though surely this was sufficient to destroy Lisa's grip on Michael.

The divorce settlement, Michael had explained, ordered him to pay all of Lisa's expenses as long as she remained in poor health. The woman she saw was no invalid.

The red Jaguar turned off ten minutes later onto an area devoted to tennis courts. Claudia felt a surge of excitement. *Are those two about to play tennis? Let me get photographs of Lisa on the tennis court! Or is she going to be a spectator?*

Claudia drove a quarter mile down the road, made a U-turn and headed back towards the tennis courts. Don't mess up now, she exhorted herself. She parked at the side of the road, reached for her camera, and walked onto the tennis court grounds. Seeming to focus on a variety of subjects, she contrived to film several of Lisa in action – plus two shots of her companion.

Her pulse racing, she returned to the car. Here it was – in her camera. The proof that Lisa was a fraud. And now, she told herself with brutal candor, she would learn if Michael – out of thrall to Lisa – still wished to have her share his life forever.

She ached to show Michael the photos of Lisa and her male companion. Undeniable proof that he was being conned. The hours until he'd return to the hotel would seem weeks! Now she debated about how to spend the intervening time.

In her mind she ran through the exhaustive research about Scottsdale. All right, she'd play the tourist scene. Find a parking lot, leave the car there and stroll about town. The weather was perfect for walking.

She visited beautiful Fifth Avenue – noted for its shops, Old Town Scottsdale – a replica of the Old West, with rustic storefronts and wooden sidewalks, and the sprawling arts district. She found a charming little restaurant where she paused for lunch.

She fretted at the delay in presenting her photos to Michael. He would approach the lawyer who'd handled the divorce, she anticipated. He would be freed of the awful burden he'd carried for years.

Moments past 5 p.m. she was back in their suite. Dress for dinner, she ordered. They were to dine at Mary Elaine's, she remembered. The food French-inspired, the service impeccable. An awesome dining experience, she gathered.

Why hadn't she packed a formal dinner dress? she reproached herself, forgetting for a moment that these had been relegated to a thrift shop. Still, the turquoise silk designer pantsuit – carefully packed to avoid wrinkling – was smart and becoming.

She changed for dinner, redid her make-up. All the while listening for the sound of Michael's return. Should she tell him right away or wait until after dinner? *Oh, how can I wait?*

As he'd expected, Michael walked into their suite minutes before 6 p.m. She searched his face – saw no answers to the questions racing across her mind.

187

Julie Ellis

'How did your day work out?' she asked solicitously after a welcoming kiss.

'I don't think this is the town for Miller's.' But he was somber.

'You were doubtful,' she reminded him. *Will Los Angeles be his next assignment? Will what I discovered today change everything for us?*

'But researching the possibility provided us with this weekend.' Now his eyes swept over her. 'You look so beautiful—'

'Michael,' she rushed ahead on sudden impulse. 'I have a confession to make.' *How can I not tell him right away?*

He pulled her close, his eyes teasing. 'You bought something wildly extravagant in a hotel shop and charged it to our suite,' he guessed.

'I had another mission,' she whispered. Her heart pounding. 'Michael, I have proof. Lisa is a fraud!'

She felt him stiffen in shock. His eyes bewildered. 'Claudia – what are you trying to say?'

Haltingly she told how she'd tracked down Lisa, called her, followed her and her companion to the tennis courts. 'You're not angry at me?' she asked in sudden alarm. *Why is he looking at me that way?*

'Angry?' His arms tightened about her. 'You're wonderful—'

'I have the photos. That business about the "cardiac test" – that was a lie,' Claudia said passionately. 'No one with a cardiac problem would have been darting about on a tennis court the way she was! Your attorney can probably check out that supposed cardiac test with the Mayo Clinic.'

'This is a miracle – and you've brought it about,' he said tenderly. 'I was too close to the situation, too unnerved, to suspect what Lisa was doing to me. I'll contact the attorney who handled the divorce. He was the one who insisted on the clause that released me from any financial obligation to Lisa if she returned to normal health.'

'Thank God for that—'

'I just wanted out of that ugly situation. The constant recriminations – that because of me her health was wrecked. That

188

I'd ruined her life. I dreaded coming home each day. I woke up each morning with a need to escape from the apartment as fast as possible.' His smile was rueful. 'I would have agreed to anything.'

'You said the New York doctors diagnosed her illness as psychosomatic,' Claudia reminded. Her face tightened. 'And it disappeared once you agreed to the divorce settlement.'

'You know what this means. Nothing – no one – can keep us apart now. I'm a free man.' His smile was dazzling. 'Claudia – once this craziness is cleared up – will you marry me?'

'Oh yes, Michael. Yes!'

'It'll take weeks – possibly months,' he warned, 'before this business with Lisa can be resolved. But it will be. How would you feel about an early spring wedding?'

'A perfect time.' *I'm not doing the rebound thing. I've waited all my life for Michael.*

At the approach of the dinner hour, they left their suite and sought out Mary Elaine's.

'What a magnificent room,' Claudia murmured when they were seated at their table in the formal, elegant restaurant. The view – a panorama of brilliant city lights – was breathtaking.

Michael's eyes made ardent love to her. 'I wish we didn't have to leave tomorrow afternoon. Damn the store!'

'You won't have to stay there,' she exulted. 'That financial behemoth will be off your back.'

'I can bear the job if we can be together on a full-time basis,' Michael said slowly.

But while they took delight in their perfect dinner – topped off with a perfect warm chocolate soufflé tart – Claudia couldn't erase from her mind the knowledge that Michael loathed his job. Without his tremendous financial obligations, must he remain at Miller's? With his background, wouldn't he able to find something less consuming? Less detested?

So many people in jobs that are their prisons!

Forty

Claudia and Michael abandoned plans to explore Scottsdale's historic sights in the Sunday hours before their afternoon flight back to New York. They lingered late in bed, packed up and headed for brunch at the Terrace Dining Room – overlooking exquisite gardens.

After brunch they checked out, drove to the airport.

'I feel as though I've died and gone to heaven,' Michael told Claudia as they waited to go through the usual airport security routine. 'I want to shout to the world that life has become beautiful.'

'You'll have to stop glowing that way,' Claudia reproached, her own face luminescent, 'or the world will know about us before we're ready to tell them.' *I'll tell Shirley – she'll be so happy for me. And I'll give Jill a hint of what's ahead. She won't think I'm jumping in too fast?*

'We'll grab a few hours sleep, then head for the salt mines,' Michael said when their plane landed at La Guardia. All at once he seemed tense. Uneasy. 'At nine thirty a.m. sharp I'll call Cliff Forbes. My attorney.'

Claudia was conscious of a new – painful – uncertainty. *He's worried that the release clause in the divorce settlement will be challenged. He said that his lawyer had wanted stronger wording about the release, but Lisa's lawyer refused to budge. Are we jumping too fast?*

In their first week back in New York Claudia and Michael strove to be confident about his divorce settlement. Neither

190

dared to express their anxiety. Both impatient that Michael must wait until Friday for an appointment with his attorney.

They were buoyed by news from the main office that the franchise holders on the Oasis – due for renewal the first of the year – would receive notice that the franchise would not be renewed. Michael was to choose a replacement, handle the changeover.

'Which means,' he interpreted, 'that I won't be shipped out to Scottsdale or Los Angeles any time soon.'

On Friday Michael left the office shortly before 10 a.m. for his meeting with Cliff Forbes. When he hadn't returned by noon, Claudia struggled to conceal her anxiety. Together they'd studied and re-studied the final divorce papers. Would the photos of Lisa be insufficient to establish the state of her health? Were she and Michael being naive about this? Did Lisa have wiggle room in the wording of the settlement?

At 1 p.m. Michael returned to his office. He paused at Claudia's cubicle. His face inscrutable.

'Let's go down to the Oasis for lunch,' he said.

'Now?' *Why doesn't he give me a hint of what's happening? Is his lawyer running into problems?*

'In five minutes. I have to make one phone call.'

As usual the Oasis was lightly populated. Michael asked for a secluded corner table.

'What did Forbes say?' Claudia asked when they were seated.

'You know lawyers.' Michael seemed tired. Dispirited. 'He didn't want me to jump to conclusions. He—'

'But the photos,' she broke in. 'There was Lisa playing tennis! *Lisa with a man who is clearly not her nurse-companion. Looking at those photos, how could anybody see her as an invalid?'*

'Forbes will arrange for a Scottsdale co-attorney. We'll get the evidence – it may take a little time.'

'But the divorce settlement will be eliminated?' she probed.

'That's the objective. I told Forbes I won't try to take back the condo – let Lisa keep it. But she must handle the mortgage and maintenance herself. I just want to be free of those staggering monthly bills.' He took a deep breath. 'The salary for her nurse-companion, the phoney medical expenses, her car—'

'What about the payments on that loan you took out?'

He grimaced in recall. 'It looks as though I'll be stuck with that. Unless I sue.' Clearly a repugnant prospect.

Their waiter approached. They focused on ordering. Alone again, Michael reached across the table for her hand.

'Forbes said he'll probably be able to scare Lisa into signing the release. If need be, he'll threaten her with criminal charges.'

'So it may take him a while.' Claudia strived for an optimistic air. 'He'll get you off the hook. And you'll escape from Miller's—'

'Claudia, I don't know.' His hand tightened on hers. 'That's security for us. I can handle it if we're together.'

For her this was a short business day, Jill thought with sardonic humor as she opened her apartment door. Barely 9 p.m. and she was home. Walking into the foyer, she realized that Chris, too, was home. A trickle of folk music was emerging from his bedroom.

'Jill?' His voice preceded him.

'No, it's the Boston Strangler.'

'What happened?' he drawled, 'For you this is practically the break of day.'

'I got disgusted,' she admitted. 'I just cut out.'

'Cool,' he approved. 'Hungry?'

'If you have something sensational in mind, I could be coaxed.' She slid out of her coat, tossed it on the sofa. 'You've been sweating over a hot stove?'

'I stopped by Citarella and picked up this luscious key lime pie.' He pantomimed eloquently.

'You brought a whole pie in this apartment?' she scolded. 'Bring it out.'

He strode towards the kitchen. 'One slice each and it goes

into the freezer. And you'll take your decaf straight – no cream, no sugar.'

While they ate with gusto, Chris turned the conversation to Taylor Publishing.

'I've been working my tail off, but I think I'm making headway.'

'Chris, you've been there just a few weeks.' Jill was skeptical.

'I've been putting out feelers – in the right direction.' He exuded confidence. 'I sense some interest. A little interest,' he amplified, 'but if I come in with the right package, they won't kick it into the slush pile. They'll listen to me.'

'Back up,' Jill ordered. 'What package?'

'The cookbook we talked about. I need a sample chapter, a rough outline. Now if your mother and Michael will—'

'Hold it right there.' Jill's mind shot back to Thanksgiving, Chris's wild idea that Mom and Michael should write a cookbook. 'Do you believe you can sell their cookbook – if they write one?'

'I told you,' he pounced, 'cookbooks are hot these days. Your mom and Michael have the right approach – a meal can be healthful and a gourmet treat at the same time. And they've got that cool patter between them. Your mother's damn good looking. Michael could set a lot of feminine hearts aflutter. They—'

'You're thinking television,' Jill broke in.

'They'd be a great TV team. With the right publicity—' He paused now. 'Of course, neither should quit their day job until we know how big the book will be.'

'You're serious.' Jill gazed at him in awe.

'Okay, so it's a gamble – but the odds are good. Get me together with those pals of yours. Diane and Zach. The publicists. They can clue me on how to set up a prospective promotion for the book. And it'll be to their advantage,' he pursued. 'If I can sell the deal, they will have made a great contact. Maybe be hired to promote the book. We'll all come out ahead.'

'Mom and Michael will think you've lost your mind,' Jill warned.

'Let's go for it,' he pushed ebulliently. 'They don't realize it, but they have a marketable product. It's up to us to persuade them. Just a sample chapter – with their flip chatter – and an outline about where the book will go. You know, categories to cover, that jazz.'

'What do you want me to do? Beside contact Diane and Zach?'

'Invite your Mom and Michael for dinner tomorrow evening,' he plotted. 'Let me take it from there.'

Forty One

Claudia glanced up from her computer as Michael strode into view. *Why does he look so strange?*

'I just had a phone call,' he said. 'From Cliff Forbes—'

'On a Saturday?' Her heart was pounding. *Had something gone wrong?*

'He was in the office to meet with an out-of-town client. His Scottsdale co-attorney called. I gather he scared the hell out of Lisa with possible felony charges. She's signed the papers.' His voice dropped to a whisper. 'I can't believe it – I'm off the hook!'

'Oh Michael!' Claudia leaped to her feet, reached to pull him close. 'How wonderful!'

'It never would have happened except for you.' He pressed his face against hers. 'My whole life changed when you walked into Miller's.'

'We're both born again,' she murmured. 'Into the life that was meant for us.'

'I can't believe it,' he reiterated. 'I'm a free man.'

Claudia glanced at her watch. 'Oh, it's later than I realized. We should be leaving soon. Remember? Dinner with Jill and Chris.'

'Right.' He struggled for calm. 'I gather dinner at Jill's will be on the informal side?'

'Undoubtedly.' *Thank God. Michael's out of bondage.*

'Then can we stop by my apartment so I can change into something more casual?' A glint of curiosity in his eyes. 'I can't figure out this dinner invitation.'

'We'll stop by your place so you can change,' she soothed. She wore gray slacks and a matching turtleneck – her Saturday attire of choice. 'And I think the dinner invitation was to show that Jill approves of our relationship.'

Michael chuckled.

He's coming out of shock.

'Smart kid.'

They left the store, stopped briefly at Michael's apartment, then headed for Jill's.

'Jill cooks,' Michael assumed as they emerged from the elevator on her floor.

'She shops,' Claudia guessed tenderly. 'At Citarella's and Zabar's.'

But approaching the apartment door they were aware of savory aromas. Claudia lifted an eyebrow. 'Jill's cooking?'

Jill opened the door for them with a dazzling smile. 'I made a marvelous discovery. Chris cooks! A limited repertoire,' she conceded. 'But talented.'

Chris was in the kitchen. A cookbook spread open on a counter.

'I'm great at following instructions.' He grinned. 'But antacids are handy in the event I go astray.'

'When did you buy that dining table and chairs?' Claudia asked. Heretofore, the dining area had offered only a bistro table and two chairs.

'They're on loan,' Jill explained. 'From the neighbors across the way. Sit and be served.'

Jill and Chris had taken into account their preference for low-fat, low-cholesterol food, Claudia noted. Chris seemed to read her mind.

'Hey, how wrong can we go with salad, chicken and garlic mashed potatoes?'

'The chicken was roasted by Citarella,' Jill conceded while they ate with relish. 'Citarella supplied the salad, too. Chris made the garlic mashed potatoes – a specialty of his mother's.'

Chris talked enthusiastically about his new job.

How wonderful – he's really excited about going to work each day.

Jill glanced about the table. Knives and forks were idle. 'Enough yakking, Chris. Let me bring on dessert.'

'It's not an evil dessert,' Chris soothed while Jill headed for the kitchen. 'Peaches stewed in Frangelico and topped with rum-raisin ice-cream. Low fat, of course.' He sighed elaborately. 'We don't have the talent of you two in coming up with gourmet recipes that don't coat your arteries and over-pad the rest of you.'

'Chris has been talking to people at Harmon & Ridgefield,' Jill plunged in, returning with dessert. 'His publishing firm,' she explained at their blank stares. 'He says he feels a lot of enthusiasm for a truly good cookbook that—'

'That fills a special need,' Chris picked up. 'Your kind of recipes.' His smile was dazzling.

'Hold it,' Claudia ordered. 'Are you two off on that track again? About Michael and me doing a cookbook?'

'You two could do it in a sensational fashion.' Chris exuded confidence. 'Look, I know there's always an element of luck involved – I'm not saying, "Quit your jobs and focus on the book." But get me a sample chapter and an outline of where it can go and—'

'Chris, we have no time to write a cookbook,' Michael rejected.

'You did that mini-cookbook for the store,' Jill reminded. 'It was great.'

196

'I can add that to the package.' Chris glowed. 'So on week-ends you can work up recipes, plan meals for the book.'

'Chris, we'd need a laboratory to check out all the recipes. Work with a dietician on calorie content. Fat content—'

'Mom, you've been testing these recipes for years! On us.' Jill turned to Michael. 'You've been trying out your recipes on yourself. You know what works!'

'The editor at Harmon & Ridgefield will help with the technical details – like putting you in touch with a dietician to analyze contents,' Chris pursued. 'No problem.'

'We have no time,' Michael dismissed this with a hungry side glance at Claudia. 'I work an eighty-hour week.'

'Cut back,' Claudia said. *Michael would love to do this – so would I.*

Michael's eyes turned to her. 'I'm not sure I can.'

But he's remembering that Lisa is off his back. That enormous financial burden doesn't exist any more. He can take a chance. Claudia felt a surge of confidence in Jill and Chris now.

'Take off the weekends, work up recipes, plan meals for the book. Give me a sample chapter and outline,' Chris repeated. 'I'll run with that. The possibilities here are tremendous. You'd both be great on TV. A cookbook and a cooking show would work great together.'

'It's a huge gamble,' Michael hedged. 'Publishers must be flooded with people who're sure they can bring in a big-selling cookbook.'

'But you two are the perfect package,' Jill joined in. She exchanged a knowing glance with Chris. 'I'll talk with Diane and Zach about a promotion campaign—'

'I'll walk in with the whole enchilada,' Chris plotted. 'Sample chapter, outline, a proposed promotion, stress the possibility of a TV cooking series –'

'Chris, how long have you been at this job?' Claudia stared at him in awe.

'Not long,' Chris admitted. 'But I went into it with heart and soul. It's what I want to do with my life,' he said passionately. 'I didn't want to be a banker – I'd have been miserable. I wanted to work in publishing, to be part of bringing books into the world.'

'I wanted to work with food,' Michael began slowly. 'Food that was good to the taste and to the body. My father convinced me there was no way I could have a restaurant. So I ended up running a department store.'

'Michael—' Claudia's voice was tremulous. 'You don't have to do that now. We won't need a huge amount of money to survive and be happy—'

'Maybe we can be a success in the food field.' Michael considered this for a moment – seeming ambivalent. He turned to Claudia. 'It's what we both want to do with our lives—'

'Yes.' Claudia's voice rang with confidence. 'We could do this book. We could do other things. Michael, we have something to offer – and the will to work at it.'

'You did it, Chris.' Something almost reverential in Michael's voice now. 'You knew – so young – where you wanted your life to take you.'

'Michael, what are you thinking?' Claudia's eyes searched his.

'I have a big bonus coming from Miller's. That'll be our security blanket if I get fired. On Monday morning I'll call Chicago. I'll make it clear I won't be transferred away from New York City. I'll stay with the company,' he said, 'as long as I need that paycheck. But we're taking time off for ourselves.'

'Michael, you can take off weekends and still handle the job,' Claudia insisted. 'We'll work on the book on weekends – any spare hours during the week that we can salvage. If you get fired, we'll manage.'

'We're rechanneling our lives, Claudia.' Michael radiated a joyous anticipation. He turned to Chris. 'You've taught us a priceless lesson.'

Claudia reached for Michael's hand, gazed lovingly at Chris and Jill. 'We'll work at something that has meaning for us. Our second chance at life.'

'Even if we don't become a real success, we'll be doing what makes us happy,' Michael said. 'Up until now I had no real hope for tomorrow.'

'Hope is what makes the world go round.' Jill glanced about the table in satisfaction. 'Who knows? I may get out of my rat race, too – if Diane and Zach still want me to work with them.'

'Wasn't it Balzac who said, "Hope is the only sin?"' Chris asked, frowning in rejection. 'He may have been a great writer – but he was a lousy philosopher.'

'The greatest sin,' Claudia said with conviction, 'is not to recognize the blessing of hope.'